THE LONG
TRAIL NORTH

THE LONG TRAIL NORTH

Robert J. Conley

Thorndike Press • **Chivers Press**
Waterville, Maine USA Bath, England

This Large Print edition is published by Thorndike Press, USA and by Chivers Press, England.

Published in 2002 in the U.S. by arrangement with Cherry Weiner Literary Agency.

Published in 2003 in the U.K. by arrangement with the author.

U.S. Hardcover 0-7862-4304-X (Western Series)
U.K. Hardcover 0-7540-8869-3 (Chivers Large Print)
U.K. Softcover 0-7540-8870-7 (Camden Large Print)

The text of this Large Print edition is unabridged.
Other aspects of the book may vary from the original edition.

Set in 16 pt. Plantin by Minnie B. Raven.

Printed in the United States on permanent paper.

British Library Cataloguing-in-Publication Data available

Library of Congress Cataloging-in-Publication Data

Conley, Robert J.
    The long trail north / Robert J. Conley.
        p. cm.
    ISBN 0-7862-4304-X (lg. print : hc : alk. paper)
    1. Cherokee Indians — Fiction. 2. Racially mixed people
— Fiction. 3. Oklahoma — Fiction. 4. Ranchers —
Fiction. 5. Revenge — Fiction. 6. Large type books.
I. Title.
PS3553.O494 L65 2002
    813'.54—dc21   2002068707

THE LONG TRAIL NORTH

Chapter

1

Dhu Walker was damn bored. The ranch was doing well. He and his two partners, Ben Lacey and Herd McClellan, had expanded their operation from just horses to horses and cattle. And they had done so primarily for show, to put up a kind of front. They had plenty of money. Money had not been a problem to them since the beginning of the LWM, since the time they had hidden away the gold they had taken from Old Harm, the renegade Confederate officer who was supposed to have been delivering it to the Confederacy but had decided to steal it for himself.

Generally speaking, the LWM partners had become well respected, if not well liked, around the area. Of course, there were still a few die-hard rebels in the territory who resented both the success of the LWM and the presence of its owners in North Texas, but most of the old hostility and animosity from the late war seemed to have died out.

Dhu sometimes wondered if he missed the excitement of the war days. He did not like to think of himself as a violent man, but he was afraid the war and its immediate aftermath had made him one. For sure, he was restless these days.

And of course there was the gnawing guilt of the expatriate. Dhu was a Cherokee, and the Cherokee Nation was his country, not Texas. It was true that he had nothing to return to in the Cherokee Nation. The war had taken his family, and he had no property. There was nothing up there for him to do. Yet he was a Cherokee, and the Cherokee Nation was having its own problems. He should be up there helping out, doing what he could. He felt just a little guilty about that.

And then there was Katharine. When Ben's parents had died up in Iowa and left his younger sister to try to manage their farm alone, Dhu and Ben had gone up there to get her, and she had come back with them to the LWM. She was a lovely young woman, hardly more than a girl, and Dhu was more than a little smitten with her, but he was unsure of his feelings, and he did not want to take unfair advantage of her innocence unless he was certain that

8

his own intentions were honorable. He was not, as yet, certain of that.

He was certain of one thing, though. Something had to happen soon. He knew that he would not be able to continue this style of living for much longer, nursemaiding a bunch of cattle and horses just to keep busy and to keep up appearances. He would have to get away and do something different, somewhere, or he would go crazy.

He rode on into town and hitched his horse in front of the general store, and then he stood and stretched before walking up onto the boardwalk and on inside.

Thane Savage was standing there at the counter buying some chewing tobacco. Dhu wondered where Savage got his money. He knew that the cowboy was unemployed, had been since the time he had tried to kill Herd's son, Sam Ed. His boss had fired him for that. Then Sam Ed had whipped Savage, and Savage had sworn that it was all over, that the feud had ended. But Dhu had his doubts about that.

Savage glanced over his shoulder to see who had come in, and when he recognized Dhu he glared. He said nothing. He just glared. Dhu could tell that the old hatred remained. Savage had hated the Mc-Clellans from the beginning. His family had been among those who had tried to run off or kill the McClellans for being northerners and Yankee sympathizers. During one such attempt Savage's uncle had been killed. That gave him another reason to hate the McClellans and everyone associated with them. Then Sam Ed had whipped Savage, whipped him bad, and Savage had lost his job over the conflict. It seemed to Dhu that Savage had plenty of reasons to keep his hatred smoldering.

In spite of all that, Dhu touched the brim of his hat and nodded when Savage looked over his shoulder, but Savage just grunted and turned back around to pick up his purchase. Then he brushed rudely past Dhu on his way out of the store. Dhu turned slightly and watched him leave. There's going to be more trouble with that one for sure, he said to himself. Sooner or later it's coming. Then a voice from behind the counter drew his attention back to the business at hand.

"Howdy, Mr. Walker. What can I do for you today?"

Dhu turned back to face the storekeeper, turning aside thoughts of Thane Savage.

"I need some saddle soap, Homer," he said.

Homer walked a few steps and turned his back long enough to reach up on a shelf for the tin. He brought it back and placed it on the counter.

"Anything else?" he asked.

"That's all," said Dhu.

"You ride all the way into town just to get a little saddle soap?" said Homer.

It did seem foolish, Dhu realized, but the truth was that he had ridden all the way into town out of his sense of restlessness and boredom. That was nobody's business, though.

"No," he said. "I'm going over to the saloon to drink a little brown whiskey."

"Well, I guess that's as good a reason as any," said Homer.

Dhu tossed some coins on the counter and picked up his saddle soap, stuffing it into a pocket.

"Thanks, Homer," he said, and he left the store. It was not very busy in Preston that day. The main street was almost deserted. Across the way a cowboy had just mounted up and was riding out of town, and a small boy rolled a hoop around the corner to chase it on down a side street. Somewhere a dog barked mournfully, and

11

just down the street from where Dhu stood, two old men sat playing checkers. Dhu stepped down off the boardwalk and headed across the street toward the saloon.

Two saddle horses were tied up to the hitch rail there, twitching their muscles and swinging their tails in a hopeless battle with the flies that pestered them. Dhu casually wondered to whom the horses belonged. When he walked inside he saw Thane Savage again. He was standing at the bar beside another young man with the look of a cowboy.

Dhu thought that it was just a look. If he was hanging out with Savage in the middle of the day, he was probably, like Savage, unemployed. There were no other customers in the place. Ignoring Savage and his companion, Dhu walked to a spot at the bar about ten feet away from them. The bartender approached him from behind the bar.

"What'll it be?" he said.

"A shot of brown whiskey," said Dhu.

"Coming up."

Dhu dug in his pocket for change, and the bartender placed a glass on the bar in front of him. Dhu paid for his drink and then took a sip. It felt good as it burned its way down to his stomach. Out of the corner of his eye he could see the two cow-boys. They seemed to have huddled a little closer together since he had come in, and they were talking in low voices. Dhu took another sip of the whiskey. He saw Savage turn sideways and lean with his right elbow on the bar to stare at him. He ignored the stare and finished his whiskey.

"One more," he said.

The bartender refilled the glass, and Dhu took another sip.

"Hey," said Savage.

Dhu ignored him.

"Hey, you. I'm talking to you," said Savage.

Dhu took another sip of whiskey.

"You Indian. Walker."

Dhu turned his head slightly to look in Savage's direction.

"You following me around?" asked Savage.

"Hell, boy," said Dhu, "I don't even see you."

"Bullshit," said Savage. "I say you're fol-lowing me."

"I'd as soon follow a stray dog," said Dhu.

"God damn you," said Savage.

"Thane," said the bartender, "don't start anything in here."

"You keep out of this," said Savage.

"You'd better listen to him," said Dhu. "He just gave you some good advice. You start anything with me, and I'll kill you before you can blink. I won't bother stomping you the way Sam Ed did. I'll just kill you. Dead."

Savage was no longer leaning on the bar. He was standing upright, braced as if for a fight, and he was trembling, but it could have been from either fear or anger. The other idle cowboy had picked up his glass and the bottle he had been sharing with Savage and backed away from the bar. Dhu was still leaning with both elbows on the bar. In his right hand he held his drink. He took another sip. If Savage was going to make a move, that was his best chance, but he did not. He stood trembling and glaring. Then suddenly he turned on his companion.

"Give me that bottle," he said, snatching it away. He moved with it back to the bar and poured himself another drink. The other cowboy, sensing that the immediate danger had passed, stepped back to the bar to stand alongside Savage. Still, he seemed apprehensive. Dhu calmly sipped his drink.

"Hey," said Savage.

"You talking to me now?" asked the bar-tender.

"Yeah, I'm talking to you. Come here."

The bartender walked toward Savage, hands on his hips and a frown on his brow.

"What is it?" he asked.

"Ain't there a law against selling liquor to Indians?"

"I don't know," said the bartender. "I've heard about them, but I don't know if we have one like that here or not. If we do, no one's ever said anything about it to me. Why?"

"That's a goddamn Indian down there, and you sold him whiskey. I think I'll report you and him both."

The bartender came up then with a large wooden mallet and swung it around and down on the bar in front of Savage with a loud thud. The glasses and the bottle in front of Savage and his comrade hopped up with the impact, and the two cowboys jumped back with a start.

"Why don't you two just pay me what you owe me and get the hell out of here?" said the mallet wielder.

"All right. All right. Come on," said Savage. "Pay the man, and let's go. This place stinks anyway."

"It was all right until you two come

15

in," said the bartender.

"Go on," said Savage. "Pay the son of a bitch."

"Hell," said the other, showing sudden panic, "I thought you was paying."

"Are you trying to stiff me?" the bartender asked, and his voice was threatening.

"No," said the cowboy. "Honest. I thought he was paying for the drinks. Hell, Thane, you invited me in here, didn't you?"

"Pay up, Savage," said the bartender.

"Well, now, I guess you'll just have to trust me for a couple of days," said Savage, feeling all of his pockets. "I don't seem to have any cash on me just now."

The bartender put the mallet back down under the bar, and Savage stood with a cocky grin on his face, but for only an instant, for the bartender came back up with a double-barreled shotgun. He pointed it at the two cowboys and pulled back both hammers.

"Shuck those sidearms," he said.

"What are you going to do?" said Savage.

"I'm going to hold them guns of yours until you pay me. That's what I'm going to do."

"Aw, come on. Wait just a minute there," said Savage. "I'll pay you. You know I'm good for it. I've spent a lot of money in here."

"Yeah," said the bartender, "back when you had a job. Now do what I said."

"Okay," said Savage, his voice beginning to betray some desperation, "just give me a little time to get some cash. I'll bring it right back."

"I'll blow your bellies through your backs if them six-guns ain't on the bar in five seconds."

"Wait a minute," said Dhu. "I'll buy their drinks. I wouldn't want these boys to get caught out somewhere unarmed. They wouldn't be able to defend themselves, would they?"

"All right," said the bartender. "Get going, then, you two, and count yourselves real damn lucky. And don't bother coming back in here, either. Neither one of you. I don't need your damn business."

Savage's face turned red, and he glared at Dhu with even more rage than before. He stood trembling for another moment. Then he turned and stamped out of the saloon, followed closely by his companion. The bartender put away his shotgun as Dhu tossed some coins up on the bar.

"You didn't make yourself no friends just then," the bartender said.

Dhu grinned. He wondered just why he had done what he had done.

"Yeah," he said. "I know."

Chapter

2

Katharine had settled into life at the LWM with ease. Her new in-laws — the McClellans — were good people, and they had accepted her with open arms and made her feel immediately like a part of the family. It was wonderful for her, too, to be around her brother again. It seemed so long to her since she had seen him, and she had been terribly lonely following the death of their parents. Her new little niece Nellie Bell had taken to her right away as well, and that made things almost perfect for Katharine. She spent much of her time with Nellie Bell, and Mary Beth didn't seem to object at all. In fact, Katharine and her sister-in-law had become great friends.

Yes, things seemed almost perfect. Almost. There was Dhu Walker. It wasn't that she was afraid of Dhu or disliked him. Quite the contrary. She found him to be a very attractive man, and she had liked him when they first met. She had even been —

well, interested. And she still felt that way. The problem was that she had thought that Dhu was also interested in her, but of late he had taken to making himself scarce, and she didn't understand why. She was puzzled by his behavior. Perhaps, she thought, she had misinterpreted his earlier attitude toward her. Perhaps she had said or done something that had offended him. After all, she had never known a real Indian before.

Dhu was a puzzle to Katharine, a mystery. She knew about his past. He had certainly not been secretive about that, but there was still something mysterious about the man. And Katharine Lacey longed to probe into that mystery and solve it.

She had on her riding clothes and was walking from the barn with a saddle, going toward the corral nearby where her favorite horse was waiting. Lunch was over, and the dishes were done. Mary Beth had taken the baby to her house to try to give her a nap. Maude was still puttering about the main house, and Herd and Ben had gone out to work. Dhu had left earlier in the day and said only that he was going to town. She had almost reached the corral when she heard a horse coming up behind her. She glanced over her shoulder to see

Ben riding up. He dismounted and walked up beside her, reaching for the saddle.

"Let me do that for you, Sis," he said.

"Thanks, Ben."

"I guess you want this on old Corker there," he said.

"Yes. He's my favorite of all of them," said Katharine.

"Well, then, he's yours."

"Mine?"

"Yeah. That's what I said. He's yours. I talked to Herd and Dhu about it, and we all agreed. Corker's yours."

"Oh, Ben, I don't know what to say. Thank you."

Katharine was so excited she was hopping up and down on her way to the corral. Ben had thrown the saddle up on a rail and was ducking under the rail to go into the corral after Corker. Katharine followed him, dancing all the way. In another few minutes Corker was saddled, and Ben gave his sister a leg up onto the horse's back.

"I'll get the gate," he said.

He moved the gate rail long enough for Katharine to ride out of the corral, and then he replaced it.

"Where you headed?" he asked.

"Oh, just out for a ride," said Katharine. "No place in particular."

"If you don't mind the company," said Ben, "I'll just ride along with you."

"I don't mind at all, but if you have other things to do, you don't have to watch over me."

Ben climbed back onto his own mount and rode over beside her.

"Naw," he said. "There ain't too much to do. Old Herd's out watching over the hands. We got enough help around here now that I could just sit back and get fat if I had a mind to. Come on."

They rode together down the lane that wound from the ranch houses nestled in the thick timber along the banks of the Red River out onto the prairie to the south. Then Katharine kicked Corker into a run across the open grassland. Ben raced behind her. After a short distance she slowed Corker back down to a walk. Ben did the same with his horse.

"Oh," she said, "that was fun. And it's even more fun somehow now that Corker is mine."

"Katharine," said Ben, "it's sure good to have you here with us."

"Ben?"

"Yeah?"

"What did Dhu say when you asked him about Corker? You know, when you asked him about giving Corker to me?"

"He said, 'Sure,' " said Ben.

"Is that all?"

"Well, not exactly," said Ben. "He didn't say much. I think he said, 'Sure. She ought to have him.' Like that."

Katharine rode on a ways in silence, seemingly deep in thought.

"Why'd you ask?" said Ben.

"Oh, I don't know. It's just that — well, Dhu seems to be acting strange lately."

"Well, I tell you what, Sis," said Ben. "Dhu's my partner and all that. We been through a lot together, and I like him just fine, but I've always thought that he was more than just a little strange-acting, and that's the truth."

"That's not what I mean," said Katharine. "When we first met — you know, when you brought him up to the farm — I thought that he — well, that he might be, you know, sort of interested in me."

"Well, yeah," said Ben, "I thought so, too. I ain't quite sure what I thought about it, though."

"Well, anyway," Katharine continued, "when we first arrived here he sat with me in the evenings some, and we even took a few walks together. He rode with me a time or two."

"Yeah," said Ben. "I know."

"Now lately he seems to be almost avoiding me, and I can't understand why."

"There ain't no telling with Dhu why he does things or why he don't," said Ben. "I give up trying to figure him out a long time ago."

"Could I have said something or done something to offend him?" she asked.

"No, I don't think that," said Ben, "and neither should you. Listen, Sis, do you want me to ask him what's wrong?"

"No!" she said sharply. "Don't you dare say a word to Dhu Walker about any of this."

"Well, okay, I won't. Hell."

"Come on," said Katharine. "I'll race you back to the house."

Thane Savage was wearing a heavy pout. He had never liked northerners, and when the problems that eventually led up to the Civil War had begun festering, he had nurtured that dislike into a full-blown hatred. During the war, though, Savage had managed to avoid conscription. He had stayed home to harass the northerners who had settled in the neighborhood. Whether it was true or not, he and his ilk had labeled these northerners — mostly Red River

24

farmers like Herd McClellan — as Yankee sympathizers, and he had taken part in the resulting violence.

Then, in an attack on the McClellan farm, his uncle had been killed. Dhu Walker and Ben Lacey had moved in with the McClellans, and they had triumphed. The war ended, and Herd McClellan's farm had developed into the prosperous and powerful LWM Ranch. Sam Ed Mc-Clellan had whipped Savage, and now the Indian Dhu Walker had embarrassed him publicly in the saloon in Preston. It was more than any man ought to have to take. And Thane Savage was not just any man.

Well, by God, he thought, he would show those Yankee bastards. He would teach them the consequences of messing with a real Texas cowboy. A gang of Yankee farmers and a goddamn Indian. Shit, he thought. By God, they'll learn the hard way. They will.

Savage and Bood Bradley, the cowboy with whom he had been drinking earlier, were hanging around their horses at the hitch rail outside of the saloon. Dhu Walker had not yet come out.

"Well, you weren't any goddamn help at all in there," said Savage.

"Hell, Thane," said Bradley, "when you

asked me to join you for a couple of drinks in there, I thought you meant you was buying. If I'd 'a' known you wasn't buying, I wouldn't have gone in with you. I been broke so damn long I forgot what money looks like."

"You could have backed my play, you little chickenshit," said Savage.

Bradley unwrapped the reins of his mount from the hitch rail and started to mount up.

"Where the hell you going?" said Savage.

"I don't know, but by God, I ain't going to hang around here and take no more abuse from you," said Bradley. He put a foot in a stirrup and grabbed the saddle-horn with both hands.

"Hold on a minute, will you?" said Savage. "I didn't mean none of that. I take it all back. Okay? I'm just pissed, is all. Now hitch that horse back up. Okay?"

"I ain't taking no more of that abuse from you," said Bradley.

"I ain't going to dish no more out. I took it all back, didn't I?"

Bradley slapped the reins back around the hitch rail.

"Well, all right," he said. "What're we going to do?"

"We're going to stand right here, and

when that damned Indian comes out the door we're going to kill him. That's what we're going to do."

"No," said Bradley. "I don't think so."

"You scared of him?"

"Someone might see us," said Bradley. "Likely they would. Right in the middle of the day like this. Right on the main street. I don't want to be accused of no murder."

Savage rubbed a hand over his face and took a few steps out into the street. Then he turned and ambled back to the hitch rail.

"Hell," he said. "You're probably right. Come on. Let's get the hell out of town."

They mounted up and rode south out of Preston. Nothing was out there. If they rode far enough, they would wind up at the headquarters of one of two large ranches. Savage had been fired from one of them not long ago, and both cowboys had applied for work at the other and been turned away. Bradley was puzzled.

"Where the hell we going, Thane?" he said.

"Old line shack out here," said Savage. "Ain't no one using it just now. It's a place to hang out."

"I know that damn place," said Bradley. "I ain't got no reason to go there."

Savage reined in his mount, and Bradley followed suit.

"Well, where the hell will you go, then?" said Savage. "You ain't got no job. Where the hell you going to go?"

"Well, I ain't sure just yet," said Bradley, scratching his head.

"Ride on out to the line shack with me, Bood, old buddy," said Savage. "We'll rest the horses, get in out of the sun, and set a spell. We need to talk some. We'll figure us out a plan of action, you and me. You with me?"

"What kind of plan?" asked Bradley.

"I don't know yet," said Savage. "I ain't going to try to tell you what to do. That's why we need to talk. Hell, buddy, if we're partners, we got to figure these things out together, you know? We got to agree on things before anybody makes any decisions or before anybody does anything. Hell, if we'd have talked like that before we went into that saloon a while ago, we wouldn't have got into no trouble. Right? That was my mistake, and I ain't going to make no mistake like that again. Are we partners?"

Bradley was clearly undecided. He wrinkled his face up in thought.

"I don't know, Thane," he said, his voice carrying a bit of a whine.

"That's all right," said Savage. "That's what I mean. We need to find us a place to set and talk things out. If we can't agree, then we ain't partners. But if we can come up with a plan by talking together, and if we both agree on things, why, then we will be partners, by God. I don't know about you, but I sure do need me a partner. Hell, I ain't got nothing else. Nothing but this old horse and my six-gun. How about you?"

"Hell," said Bradley, "I ain't got nothing either. I never did want too much. Just a job of work, but I can't even get that around here. I was thinking of pulling out. Maybe going north. Up to Montana or Wyoming or someplace like that. I ain't never been up thataway, but I hear there's big ranches up there. There ought to be lots of jobs."

"How you going to get up there broke?" said Savage.

"I don't know."

"Well, you see? This is just the way we ought to be talking about things, but not out here in the middle of nowhere like this, sitting in the saddle under the hot sun. How about that line shack?"

"All right," said Bradley. "Let's go."

Chapter

3

They had just finished breakfast, and the women were clearing off the table and getting ready to wash the dishes. The men headed out of the main house: Dhu, Ben, Sam Ed, old Herd, and the three cowboys who worked for them.

"Herd," said Ben, "we're going to have to do something about that kitchen pretty soon. Maude's pretty crowded in there feeding this bunch."

"Yeah, I know it," said Herd. "She's a good woman, Maude. She mentioned it once. Ain't fussed about it to me since then. Let's get on it first thing tomorrow. These boys can handle the ranch work for a few days without us."

They stepped down off the porch, and Herd glanced toward the corral.

"Damn," he said. "He's done it again."

"What?" said Sam Ed.

"Clabber has knocked down that gate rail again, and them horses are all out of the corral. No telling where they've got off to."

"Well," said Dhu, "let's go find them."

The horses that the men intended to ride that morning had all been stabled in the barn. The corral had held some that needed some working. Sure enough, the corral was empty. The men went to the barn and saddled their mounts.

"Sam Ed," said Herd, "you and the boys go down by the river. Me and Ben and Dhu will ride out toward the prairie and check there."

"Sure thing, Pa," said Sam Ed, and he led the three cowhands toward the river. Dhu was already headed south toward the prairie. Herd and Ben followed. At the end of the lane Dhu turned east.

"Go on along with Dhu," Herd said to Ben. "I'm going this other way."

He turned west, riding along the timberline. Not far ahead of Herd, Thane Savage and Bood Bradley lay hidden in the trees.

"Someone's coming," said Bradley.

"I knew letting them horses out would bring them out," said Savage. "Sneak a look. How many is they?"

Bradley crept out a few feet and peeked from around a tree. He waited a few seconds, then scooted back.

"Just one," he said. "It looks like the old man."

Savage pulled out his six-gun, checked the load again, and thumbed back the hammer.

"What you going to do, Thane?" said Bradley.

"Just what I said. What we talked about. I'm going to kill the old son of a bitch."

"I thought you meant the Indian," said Bradley.

"It's all the same, ain't it? Now shut up. He'll hear us."

They lay still, listening to the sounds of the approaching horse and rider. Then, when he could see him close through the thicket, Savage stepped out into Herd's path, his gun drawn and aimed. Herd opened his mouth as if to speak, but he didn't have time. Savage pulled the trigger, and lead tore through Herd's chest. His body jerked, and his horse jumped and bolted. Herd stayed in the saddle for a short run, then fell off backwards and landed with a thud. He didn't move.

"Come on," said Savage. "Let's make sure he's dead."

"We got to get out of here," said Bradley.

"We will," said Savage. "Just as soon as I make sure. You go get the horses."

Savage ran toward where Herd lay still, and Bradley went back into the woods. When Bradley emerged from the woods leading two horses, Savage was about halfway to Herd. But Bradley picked up another sound from behind him. He looked over his shoulder toward the east.

"Riders coming," he shouted, and he kicked his horse, racing toward Savage. As the two horses came up alongside him Savage grabbed his own saddlehorn and made a running mount, and the two raced away.

Dhu was the first one on the scene. He saw the two riders off in the distance, and he thought that he might be able to catch them, but he also saw Herd McClellan lying there on the ground. He had a moment of painful indecision, then he dismounted and ran to Herd's side, dropping down on his knees. Ben came up then, and he, too, dismounted.

"Is he dead?" said Ben.

"No," said Dhu, "but he's hit bad. I'll stay here and try to stop the bleeding. You go get the buckboard. Hurry now."

Ben jumped back on his horse and raced away toward the house and barn. Dhu pulled the handkerchief out of his back pocket and stuffed it into the hole in

Herd's chest in an attempt to stop the bleeding. Herd groaned.

"Hang on, Herd," said Dhu. "Hang on. Ben's bringing the buckboard. We'll get you back to the house."

"I seen the bastard," said Herd.

"It's all right, Herd," said Dhu. "Just keep quiet. We'll talk later."

"Hell," said Herd. "I might die. I tell you, I seen him. Face to face."

"Who was it?"

"Savage."

"Thane Savage?" said Dhu. "I could have guessed it. I promise you one thing, Herd. He won't get away with it. I'll get him for you if it's the last thing I ever do. You've got my word on that. Now try to rest easy. Okay?"

"Yeah. Yeah," said Herd. "You get the little skunk for me, Dhu. Get him, you hear me? God damn it to hell."

Ben came back with the buckboard, and he and Dhu loaded Herd into it and took him back to the ranch house. They got him inside and into bed, and Maude went to work. She cut and tore the shirt off Herd's back and examined the wound. The bullet had gone all the way through. Maude washed both the entrance and exit wounds with cold water. Then she applied soot to both to work as a styptic to stop the bleeding. Finally she bound the wounds up tight with clean cloth.

There was no need to send out for a doctor. They all knew that there was none to be found near enough to do any good. They were all also confident that Maude would do everything that could possibly be done. When Maude was finished, at least for the time being, and Herd was sleeping, Dhu put his hat back on his head and started for the door.

"Where you going, Dhu?" asked Ben.

"I'm going after Thane Savage," said Dhu.

"Is he the one who done this?" said Sam Ed.

"He's the one," said Dhu. "Herd told me."

"I'm going with you," said Sam Ed.

"Me, too," said Ben.

"No, you're not," said Dhu. "There's still work to be done around here. Herd would be the first one to tell us that. Besides that, we don't know what Savage will try next, and," Dhu hesitated a second, "we don't know how many might be with him. We can't leave the house and the women unprotected."

"Then you stay here," said Sam Ed,

"and let me go after Savage."

"Herd told me to do it," said Dhu, "and I promised him that I would."

There was no more argument. Dhu left alone. He went back to the spot where he had found Herd lying on the ground, where he had seen the two riders racing off, and he tried to follow the tracks, but he soon gave up that idea. The tracks disappeared out on the dusty grassland. He headed for Preston. They might not be there, but it was a place to start.

Dhu knew that Savage was unemployed. He did not know where the man had been staying since he lost his job. He wondered if the other unemployed cowboy, the one he had seen with Savage in the saloon, had been the second rider. He guessed that it was probably so, but of course he couldn't be sure. He hadn't really gotten a good look at them as they rode away. But who else had Savage been hanging out with lately? He couldn't think of anyone. Most of Savage's old cronies still had their jobs.

Dhu thought that he would ride into Preston and take a quick look around. If he saw no sign of Savage, he would start to ask around to see if anyone had seen the man. That was his plan. But when he reached the town the first thing he saw was a small crowd gathered in front of the saloon. He rode to a near hitching rail, dismounted, tied his horse, and joined the crowd to see what was going on. Right away he noticed that the sheriff from over at the county seat was there. Everyone seemed to be talking at once. Dhu glanced over the crowd, and he spotted Homer from the general store. He stepped over beside him and nudged him with an elbow.

"What's going on here, Homer?" he asked.

"Hi, Walker," said Homer.

"What's going on?"

"Joe Morgan's dead," said Homer.

"Joe? The bartender?"

"That's right. Billy Bob Hamman noticed this morning that the saloon was still open. It don't open till afternoon, you know. So he went inside, and he found Joe in there dead."

"How'd it happen?" Dhu asked.

"Beat to death, it looks like. His head's busted in. So anyhow, Billy Bob rode on over to Gainesville to get the sheriff."

"Do they know who did it?" said Dhu.

"No idea," said Homer. "We figure, though, that whoever it was came in just about closing time — just when Joe was kicking everyone out, you know — and when all the other customers was gone, whoever it was killed poor old Joe and stole his cash. That's the way we got it figured."

Dhu thought a moment, then pushed his way through the crowd to stand beside the sheriff.

"George," he said, "can I talk to you for a minute?"

"I'm pretty busy here, Walker," said George McGee, the county sheriff. "We had us a killing here last night."

"That's what I want to talk to you about," said Dhu.

"You know anything about this?"

"I'm not sure. I might. Can we talk in private?"

McGee and Dhu extricated themselves from the crowd and walked down the street where they could talk alone. McGee pulled a cigar out of his vest pocket, struck a match, and lit the cigar.

"All right, Walker," he said, "what do you know?"

"I was in the saloon yesterday," Dhu said. "Thane Savage was drinking with another out-of-work cowboy. I don't know the other one's name. Anyhow, Savage tried to start a fight with me, and I wouldn't have any of it. Joe finally tossed Savage out. Savage left pretty mad."

"Is that all?" said McGee.

"No, sir," said Dhu. "It's not. This morning out at the LWM Savage ambushed Herd McClellan. Shot him in the chest from up close. I came up just as they were riding away. I didn't get a good look at them, but Herd told me it was Savage who shot him."

"How bad hit is McClellan?" asked the sheriff.

"It's bad enough, but he's still alive. He might pull through."

"Well," said McGee, "that don't prove that Savage killed Joe Morgan, but we can get him for attempted murder on McClellan. From what you've just told me, I'd bet he done this killing here, too."

"That would be my guess," said Dhu. "What do you do now?"

"Try to find old Thane and arrest him," said McGee. He turned and started walking back toward the saloon. Most of the crowd was still there, waiting to find out what Dhu Walker had told the sheriff. As McGee and Dhu got closer McGee spoke out.

"Any of you boys seen old Thane Savage around today?"

"Not today," said Homer, and several others agreed.

"Who's he been running with lately?"

"He's been chumming around with an old boy named Bood Bradley," said one of the men in the crowd. "Bood's a cowboy, like Thane. Out of work like him, too."

"Say," said another, "do you think Thane and Bood done this to old Joe?"

"I don't know," said McGee, "but Savage shot Herd McClellan this morning, and he had an argument with Joe yesterday. We need to find him."

"Sheriff," said a cowboy, "I seen them two yesterday evening out at the old line shack south of town."

"Can you show me where?" said McGee.

"Right now?" asked the cowboy.

"You know a better time?"

"I reckon not," said the cowboy. "Just let me go get my horse."

"I'm coming along," said Dhu.

McGee looked at Dhu and chewed on his cigar.

"I got no objection," he said. "Come on. Let's ride."

At the line shack they found a little evidence that someone had been there in the last few days, but they did not find Thane Savage or Bood Bradley, and they did not find any real evidence that the shack's recent inhabitants had been those two. They had for that information only the word of the cowboy. And they did not find any indication of the direction the shack's two late inhabitants might have taken. The trip out to the line shack had gotten them nowhere.

"What now?" said Dhu.

"Well," said McGee, "the word's out on them two now. Someone'll see them somewhere. They ain't too many places they can go around here, you know."

"No," said Dhu, "but they can leave the country."

"They'll have to pass through somewhere to do it," said the sheriff. "We'll hear about it. You might as well go on back to your ranch. I'll get word to you when I find out anything."

"I'm going after Thane Savage, Sheriff," said Dhu. "I'll let you know when I get him."

Chapter
4

Dhu rode back into Preston and looked the whole town over. He went into every business establishment, knocked on every door. There was no sign of Thane Savage or of Bood Bradley. No one could tell him anything more about either one of them. He rode over to Gainesville and went through the same thing there. Savage and Bradley seemed to have disappeared. Of course, Texas was wide-open country. They could have gone in any direction. But what was logical? They had killed a man, maybe two, if Herd didn't make it. Dhu figured that meant they would hightail it out of the country, but in which direction?

If they were wanted for murder in Texas, it stood to reason that they would try to get out of Texas. That meant they would cross the Red River and ride into Indian territory. It was the only thing that made any sense to Dhu, but the only problem was that he wasn't at all certain that either

Savage or Bradley had the sense to reason that all out. Those damn fools might just ride right back into Preston. Still, it was the only idea he had. He rode to Colbert's Crossing on the Red River, just a short ride west of the road to the LWM. The ferry was tied up on the other side of the river.

"Hey, Colbert," he shouted.

The lanky form of Colbert peered out the door of his dirty, tattered old canvas tent.

"Is that Dhu Walker calling?" he said, squinting and walking toward the river.

"Yes, it is. Come across and get me, if that raft of yours will still float."

Colbert reeled his raft across by the lines that were tied from one shore to the other. Dhu left his horse and rode the raft across. In a few minutes he was sitting cross-legged in the dirt with Colbert in front of the tent, drinking hot coffee out of a tin cup.

"I hear tell you boys is doing real well over there on the other side," said Colbert.

"I got no complaints," said Dhu. "How about you?"

"Aw," said Colbert, "business is slow. You're the first fare I've had in a week, and I ain't going to charge you."

"I don't mind paying you," said Dhu.

"Nope. I swore that you boys would ride free from now on, ever since you saved me from them renegade rebels. You think I'd forget that? Hell, man, I don't forget a promise."

"No," said Dhu. "Of course you don't."

He glanced up and over the tent to look at the framework and front wall still standing back there unfinished. The boards looked weathered and old. The first time he had seen them, they had looked new.

"I'd have thought that by now you'd have your house finished," he said.

"I guess I just ain't been much motivated lately," said Colbert. "But what the hell are you doing here, Dhu? You didn't come up here just to visit with me, did you? Not that you ain't welcome, mind."

"No," said Dhu. "I didn't. Could I have a little more of that coffee?"

Dhu held out his cup, and Colbert poured it full again.

"It'll grow hair on your chest, won't it?" he said.

"Thanks. Yeah, it is pretty stout. I'm looking for two men," said Dhu. "They killed a bartender in Preston, and they shot my partner, Herd McClellan."

"Kill him?"

44

"He's still alive," said Dhu, "but he's in a bad way. We can't tell yet if he's going to make it or not. But either way, I promised Herd I'd get them."

"Kill them?"

"That's what I mean to do."

"And you think they might've crossed here?"

"I don't know. I can't find a trail anywhere."

"Well, like I said before, it's been a week since anybody's crossed over here, Dhu," said Colbert, "but if you'll tell me what to look for, I'll keep my eyes peeled."

"They're two cowboys," said Dhu. "Out of work. The leader is named Thane Savage. I'd guess he's about twenty-five or twenty-six years old. Medium height. Stocky. Red hair and watery blue eyes. His partner, Bood Bradley, is about the same age. Maybe younger. Tall and lanky. Not quite as tall as you. Brown hair and green eyes. I expect that they're both kind of ratty-looking just now. You know, dirty clothes and a little ragged. They're packing guns, and they're itchy to use them. Especially Savage. If they come around, be careful. Don't try anything. Just wait until they're gone and get word to me."

"I ain't no hero," said Colbert. "Just a businessman. I'll do like you say."

"Oh, yeah," said Dhu. "One more thing. If you do see those boys, try not to talk about the war, and if they bring up the subject, play like you're a disgruntled rebel. They hate Yankees, and they have long memories."

"I'll remember," said Colbert. "I play them kind of games like a real actor."

The day was almost done, and Dhu rode back to the LWM. He went past his own little cabin and on down to the main house. Ben was sitting on the porch. Dhu climbed down out of his saddle and hitched his horse to the porch rail.

"How's Herd?" he asked.

"No change," said Ben. "He just lays there. He's breathing, but that's all."

"Is everyone else inside?"

"Mary Beth took the baby over to our house to put her to bed," said Ben. "Everyone else is in there with Herd. Maude and Katie and Sam Ed."

Dhu sat down on the edge of the porch and reached in his shirt pocket for the makings of a cigarette. He held them out toward Ben.

"No, thanks," said Ben.

Dhu busied himself rolling a smoke, and then he lit it, drew in a lungful, and let it out slowly.

"Ben," he said, staring into the dissipating cloud of blue-gray smoke, "I'm riding out of here in the morning."

"Riding out?" said Ben. "What do you mean? Where to?"

"I made a promise to Herd, and I'm going to keep it if I can," said Dhu. "I'm going after Thane Savage and his partner."

"But you don't know where he's at, do you?"

"No, I don't, and I won't find out sitting around here."

"Where will you look?" asked Ben.

"I figure they went north, across the river. They'll be wanted for murder here in Texas, and that's the fastest way out of the state. I'll start out by riding the river to see if I can find out where they might've crossed over."

"Likely they crossed at Colbert's," said Ben, "if they crossed at all."

"I've already been there," said Dhu. "Colbert hasn't seen them."

They sat for a long moment in silence. Dhu smoked his cigarette down until he didn't have anything left to hold onto, and he tossed it aside.

"And what if you don't find nothing?" said Ben.

"Then I just ride north and keep looking for them," said Dhu. "I'll find them somewhere, sometime, sooner or later."

He was ready early in the morning. Extra clothes, food, and plenty of ammunition were stuffed into his saddlebags, and a blanket roll was tied on behind the saddle. He carried two revolvers and a long hunting knife in his belt and a rifle in a saddle boot. Under his shirt he wore a money belt with all the cash he thought that he'd need for a long journey. He had hoped that he would be able to leave quietly, but such was not the case.

Leading his horse out of the corral, he saw Ben and the McClellans gathered around Herd's porch waiting for him. Leading his horse, he took off his hat and walked over to the small gathering.

"Dhu," said Ben, "you sure you want to go this alone?"

"I'm sure, Ben," said Dhu. "I don't even know where I'm going."

He glanced at Maude.

"How's Herd doing?" he asked.

"No change, Dhu," she said, "except that he seems to be resting a bit easier. I know what he said to you, and I know you made a promise, but you don't really have to do this."

"I'm going, Maude," said Dhu.

"I want to go along with you," said Sam Ed. "It's because I whipped him that Thane Savage shot my daddy. I ought to go along."

"No," said Maude.

"You stay here with your mother, Sam Ed," said Dhu. "I know how you feel, boy, but look at it from where your mother stands. If your daddy doesn't pull through, you'll be all she's got left. Don't argue. Stay here. I'll take care of it for you."

Then he heard soft footsteps behind him, and he turned to see Katharine Lacey coming from Ben's house. She stopped when he turned. She stood there for a moment and looked at him. They were close enough to have touched had they both reached out their arms, but, of course, they didn't.

"Dhu," she said, "be careful."

He rode the river, checking for all the places a man on horseback might cross without too much trouble. The first one was the ford on their own property — the place where, a few years back, they had ambushed Old Harm and taken the gold. It was still fordable, but he found no evidence that anyone had crossed there recently. He hadn't really expected anything, but he thought he should check it just in case. He rode into the low water, crossed to the Indian Territory side, and turned his horse west. He thought that there were a couple of other possible crossings down that direction.

Where the river was too high for crossing he found that his mind was wandering. He didn't have to concentrate on looking for sign, and so his thoughts went back to the LWM and the friends he had just said good-bye to. He thought about Ben Lacey, the ignorant Iowa farm boy fate had attached to him. If he had met Ben under normal circumstances, he thought, he would never have bothered getting to know him. As it was, he had not liked him. But they had been forced by the situation they had been in at the time to stick together for a while, and now they were partners. He hesitated, even in his private thoughts, to say "friends," and that hesitation made him feel a little bit guilty. He shrugged it off.

And he thought of Maude and of Sam Ed, a wife and a son waiting anxiously to find out whether Herd would live or die. They were good people, the McClellans, and they had been forced to put up with more trouble in their lives than was fair. Then he thought of his own Cherokee people, and he gave a little smirk. Nothing about life was fair. You just had to get through it the best way you could. That was all.

But then there was Katharine. That was real irony, Dhu thought. There had been plenty of times over the last few years when Dhu had wished he had never met Ben Lacey. But now, he thought, if he had not met Ben, he would certainly never have met Ben's sister, and she was quite a young woman. He was glad that he knew her. He recalled her brief farewell to him that morning.

"Be careful," she had said. Nothing more. She hadn't begged him not to go or urged him to hurry back. Just "be careful." That was all. That gave him just one more thing to like about her. One more thing to — love? No. That was another word he was hesitant to use. He pushed these thoughts out of his mind when he saw that he was approaching Colbert's Crossing.

"Two days in a row," said Colbert when he saw Dhu riding up. "Well, climb on down."

Dhu dismounted, and Colbert poured the coffee.

"What you doing riding up on this side?" he said.

"Checking the fords," said Dhu. "Are there any places on west of here where a man could ride across?"

"Just one I can think of," said Colbert. "About two miles, I'd say. There's a big cottonwood there that leans way out like it's trying to stretch on across the river. You can't miss it."

He didn't stay long with Colbert. He finished one cup of old, stale coffee, then headed on west along the river looking for the big cottonwood. When he found it he discovered a sure-enough ford, but again there was no evidence of a recent crossing.

"Damn," said Dhu. Could they still be in Texas? It didn't make sense. But if they had left the state, where did they cross the river? He wasn't sure where to go next. He hadn't found where they had crossed the river, yet he was almost sure that they had crossed. There was no reason for them to stay in Texas, and no place for them to hide. The old line shack where they had been staying had been checked out, as had all the nearby towns. No one had seen them. They must have gone into Indian territory.

Dhu could think of nothing else to do, so he turned his horse northeast. He didn't want to bother with Colbert again so soon, so he rode around the ferryman's establishment and found his way back down to the road. He was headed for the Cherokee Nation. He was headed for home.

Chapter

5

It took Dhu Walker eleven days to ride to the home of Middle-striker in the Cherokee Nation near the Arkansas border. He thought it had been eleven days, but he wasn't really quite sure. He might have lost count somewhere along the way. He pulled up in front of the house and reined in his mount to wait, but Middle-striker had heard his approach and came out the door. A smile spread across the dark face of the full-blood Cherokee.

" '*Siyo*, Inoli," said Middle-striker, greeting Dhu in Cherokee and calling him by his Cherokee name.

" '*Siyo*, my friend," said Dhu. He also spoke in Cherokee, for Middle-striker knew no English, and Dhu thought that it felt good to be speaking again in his native tongue.

"Get down," said Middle-striker, "and come inside."

Middle-striker's log cabin was small but

sturdily built. Inside, it was one large room with a huge fireplace on the north wall. The only door opened to the east. The cabin was furnished with homemade, hand-hewn furniture. There was a dining table and four chairs, and against the south wall was a bed. Another bed was on the loft overhead. There were no stairs. A ladder led up to the loft.

Dhu had smelled the beans cooking from outside even before he had climbed down off his horse, but inside the aroma was thick, and Dhu's hunger suddenly seemed acute. There was a woman bending over the pot at the fireplace. She turned to look at Dhu when he stepped in.

"Do you know my wife?" asked Middle-striker. "I think she was away when you were here before. This is Egi."

"*Osiyo,*" said Dhu.

"Egi," said Middle-striker, "this is Inoli. I've told you about him before. You remember."

Egi smiled and nodded.

"Yes," she said. "Come in and sit down. You're welcome here, Inoli. These beans will be ready to eat soon."

Dhu sat down at the table.

"*Wado,*" he said, thanking her for the invitation.

"Kawis jaduli?" said Middle-striker, reaching for the coffeepot, which was precariously balanced on a log at a far edge of the fire.

Dhu nodded affirmatively.

"Yes," he said. "Coffee would be real good right now."

Middle-striker poured steaming black coffee into two tin cups and placed the cups on the table, one in front of Dhu. He replaced the coffeepot, then moved back to the table and sat across from Dhu.

"It's good to see you, Inoli," he said.

"It's good to see you," said Dhu, "and to meet your wife at last."

Egi glanced over her shoulder and smiled, then went on with her work.

"We have a son," she said, "but he's not at home just now."

"No," said Middle-striker. "He's out hunting."

He smiled slyly, raised a fist up in front of his face and slowly and suggestively straightened his index finger until it curved slightly upward.

"He's at that age, you know," he said.

Dhu chuckled.

"I understand," he said, and he thought about Katharine Lacey, and the thought embarrassed him. He had a peculiar feeling that Middle-striker could read his thoughts. He picked up the cup and sipped some coffee. It was hot, slightly bitter, and it tasted good. Better, Dhu thought, than his own trail brew.

Egi ladled beans from the black kettle into bowls and put the bowls on the table. Then she handed spoons around, and Dhu and Middle-striker started to eat. Egi was still busy, though. She produced a platter of bean bread, which she set in the middle of the table, and she refilled the coffee cups. Finally she sat down to eat.

After the meal was done Dhu leaned back from the table, feeling the tightness of the belt around his waist.

"*Wado*," he said to Egi. "It was good. I haven't eaten so well in a long time. I've been living with white people."

They all laughed, and Dhu felt a little guilty at the joke he had made at the expense of his friends back in Texas. Then, at Middle-striker's suggestion, the two men went outside to sit and smoke and visit.

"Pretty soon it will be too cold for this," said Middle-striker. "Winter will be here soon."

"Yes," said Dhu. "Pretty soon. But just now it's pleasant."

There was already a slight chill in the

evening air. The leaves around had all turned red and yellow and brown, and some were falling off the trees.

"It's colder here than it is where I've been living," Dhu said. He noticed that he couldn't bring himself to refer to Texas as home.

"How is your weather there?" asked Middle-striker.

"Mostly hot and dry," said Dhu.

"And the people," said Middle-striker. "Are they all white people where you live?"

"Yes," said Dhu. "They tell me that there are some Indians around. Plains people. They say that they come around now and then, but I haven't met any of them."

"Comanches?" asked Middle-striker.

"Yes," said Dhu, "and some Kiowas and Cheyennes, I guess. Some Wichitas."

"Those Comanches will steal your horses," said Middle-striker. "I've talked to some Chickasaws who said that Comanches stole their horses."

"If they come around, then," said Dhu, "I'll be careful of them. I'll watch my horses."

They sat for a long moment in silence, Middle-striker puffing his pipe, Dhu rolling and lighting another cigarette.

"I'm looking for someone," said Dhu, "and I need some help. I need to see a knower."

Middle-striker puffed on his pipe and looked thoughtful. For an instant smoke clouded his face, giving him a look of mystery in the evening twilight.

"In the morning," he said, "we'll go see Yellow Hammer. He's my uncle. Tonight you can stay here." He puffed his pipe some more, and then he added, "He can do that."

Herd McClellan was awake. He had talked very little, for he was weak from loss of blood, but Maude had propped up his head on pillows and was feeding him a strong beef broth.

Outside Sam Ed was sitting on the porch smoking a cigarette. Maude didn't approve of his smoking, so he didn't do it in the house. Ben Lacey stepped out of his own small house across the way, saw Sam Ed, and walked over to the main house.

"Howdy, Ben," said Sam Ed. "Smoke?"

"No, thanks," said Ben. "How's your daddy doing?"

"A lot better. Ma's feeding him some broth right now. He's still awful weak, but by God, Ben, the old man's going to pull through. He's tougher'n hell, that old man. You know that?"

"Yeah," said Ben. "I know that. They don't make them no tougher than old Herd. Has he said anything?"

"Well, not much," said Sam Ed. "Whenever he first come out of it, the first thing he said was, he said, 'I ain't dead.' That's just what he said. Me and Ma was sitting at the table eating, and we just barely heard him, his voice was so low. 'I ain't dead,' he said. Boy, we jumped up and run right over there. 'What did you say?' said Ma. And he said it again. 'I ain't dead,' he said."

"Yeah," said Ben. "I remember that. He ain't said much since then?"

"Not much," said Sam Ed. "He sleeps a lot, and when he wakes up he's hungry. Ma feeds him, and he's wore out again and goes back to sleep. That's about it. But he's getting stronger every day. I know he is. He's going to pull through this, Ben. He is."

Ben sat down on the edge of the porch and stared off down the lane that stretched out away from the houses, through the thicket, to the edge of the LWM land, and out onto the prairie.

"Let me have a smoke," he said.

"Sure," said Sam Ed, and he handed the makings to Ben. Ben laboriously rolled himself a cigarette, handed the makings back to Sam Ed, and lit his smoke. It flared up for an instant on the end, but then it drew all right. He couldn't roll them as well as Dhu Walker or even as well as Sam Ed, and he felt a twinge of jealousy as he exhaled his first lungful of smoke. It felt harsh to his throat. He didn't smoke very often.

"I wonder where that damn Indian is at," he said.

"Yeah," said Sam Ed. "I wonder where that goddamn Thane Savage is at."

"Well," said Ben, taking another drag on the cigarette, "I bet you one thing. I bet you Dhu Walker finds him."

"That'd be a sucker bet," said Sam Ed, "but I just wish that he'd took at least one of us along with him. That's all."

"Yeah," said Ben. "Me, too."

Not many miles away at a litter-strewn primitive campsite beside the river, just a mile or so west of the big cottonwood beyond which Dhu Walker had not searched, four cowboys were breaking camp. Bood Bradley poured the dregs from a coffeepot onto the campfire. The

61

fire sizzled but did not go out.

"Where we going, Thane?" he said.

"We got to get out of Texas," said Savage. "You and me're wanted for murder."

"That old Yankee didn't die," said Bradley. "They say he's still hanging on. That's what these boys said."

"Yeah," said Savage, "but that bartender is deader'n hell, and what it all adds up to is we're wanted for murder and for attempted murder, and if they catch us now, they'll hang us for both."

"You mean they'll hang us twice?" said Bradley.

"Hell," said Savage, "they might. Damn Yankee carpetbagger laws."

"You probably won't mind the second time," said one of the other two cowboys.

"Maybe not," said Savage, "but I'd rather not experience the first one. Get all that stuff packed up now, and let's get out of here."

"Thane," said Bradley, "George McGee ain't no Yankee carpetbagger. He's a Texan. I know he is. And he was even in the Confederate army."

"Aw, shut up," said Savage. "I don't give a shit about George McGee."

For an instant a pout crossed Bood

Bradley's face, but it vanished with his next thought.

"We going across the river, Thane?" he asked.

"That's the quickest way to get the hell out of Texas, ain't it?" said Savage. "Hurry up now. Get packed and saddled up. I ain't going to feel none too good again until we're over there on the other side of this Red River in that damn Indian Territory."

"Will there be a bunch of redskins over there, Thane?" asked Bradley.

"How the hell would I know?" said Savage. "I ain't never been over there before. I reckon there will be, though, otherwise why'd they call it Indian Territory?"

"Thane?" said Bradley.

Savage looked up, exasperated, from the cinch he was tightening.

"What?" he said.

"What're we going to do in the Indian Territory?"

For a moment Savage seemed calmer, serious, and more concerned. He leaned one arm on the saddle on his horse's back.

"I hear tell that some of them Indians up there got banks," he said. "Just like white men. They call them 'civilized Indians,' you know. That's the reason. 'Cause they got banks. Well, I'm kind of thinking that we just might rob us a bank in Indian Territory. Then we can ride out of there, either into Arkansas or into Kansas, depending on where we find us a bank. Right now, though, we got to load up and get across that river."

"This looks too deep here," said Bradley, tossing a saddle on a horse's back and looking over his shoulder toward the river. "Do you think we can cross here?"

"Not without getting good and wet, we can't," said the other cowboy, the one who had spoken before. "There's places where we can cross, though. I know a couple of them not far from here."

The fourth cowboy had not yet said a word. He had eaten in silence, packed in silence, and saddled his horse in silence. He listened to the others and watched them with cold eyes.

"We ain't going to wade across no water," said Savage. "We're going on down to the ferry. I've heard tell there's quicksand in this damn river, and I ain't taking no chances."

"I wouldn't want to get sucked down in no quicksand either," said Bradley.

In another few minutes the four cowboys were mounted up. They rode off, Thane

Savage in the lead, lashing his horse with a quirt, leaving the refuse of their camp scattered about, the abandoned campfire still smoldering.

Chapter
6

"Are they white men?" Yellow Hammer asked, speaking in Cherokee. He was sitting on an old straight-backed, cane-bottomed chair beneath an arbor that stood a few feet away from his cabin, a cabin much like that of Middle-striker. Underneath the arbor were a variety of pots and baskets, most of them containing dried plants, and plants in various stages of drying were suspended from all four of the arbor roof's frame poles. Dhu sat across from Yellow Hammer in a chair practically identical to the one in which the old "knower" sat. A small fire burned on the ground between them.

"They're all white men," said Dhu. "The man who was killed, my friend who was shot, and the killers."

"Hmm," murmured Yellow Hammer, and he just sat, apparently in deep thought, for a long moment of silence. Dhu sat and waited. Then Yellow Hammer picked up a clay pipe with a short river-cane stem that had been lying on top of a wooden keg beside his chair. The pipe bowl was adorned with a small carved or molded figure. From where Dhu sat he couldn't be sure, but he thought that it was a turtle. A tobacco pouch was there, too, on the keg, and Yellow Hammer picked that up as well and filled the pipe bowl. Then he half stood and stretched with a groan. He reached down to the fire, picked up a burning stick, and used it to light his pipe. He replaced the stick, sat back in his chair again, and smoked.

Now and then Dhu glanced up to get a brief look at Yellow Hammer. He was a young man for his profession, perhaps in his mid-fifties. His long, gray-streaked hair was combed straight and loose and flowed over his shoulders, down his back, and down over his chest. He wore deerskin moccasins on his feet, but his trousers and flannel shirt were store-bought. His hunting jacket, of once brightly colored stripes, long since faded, was clearly homemade. He wore a thin mustache that ran down the corners of his mouth almost to his jawline. He looked up through a cloud of smoke at Dhu, just briefly. Then he looked away.

"Usually," he said, "I go to a person's

home or wherever it was that the person lost the thing he is looking for. Now I can't do that. Wait for me here, and I'll be back."

He stood up and walked out of the arbor and across the way to his house. Then he went inside. Dhu waited a short while. When he began to feel impatient he took out the makings of a cigarette and rolled himself a smoke. He lit it with a stick from Yellow Hammer's fire, and he sat back down to smoke.

The cigarette had been out for a few minutes when Yellow Hammer returned. His right fist was clenched. He came back into the arbor and sat down again. Holding his fist, palm up, out in front of himself, he slowly opened it up. There was a smooth brown stone and a wad of string.

Yellow Hammer carefully untangled the string and found its loose end. He took the end of the string between the thumb and forefinger of his left hand and lifted it until Dhu could see that the stone was suspended from the other end. Yellow Hammer stilled the dangling stone with his right hand and stared at it.

"Listen to me, Brown Rock. You have just come here to hear me. He has come here for my help," he said. "His name is

Inoli, and he has lost something. It is a man he is looking for. A white man named Savage. A killer. Inoli is looking for this white man.

"You never tell a lie. Now tell me where Inoli can find this white man, this killer. My name is Yellow Hammer."

As Dhu watched, the rock on the end of the string began to swing. Yellow Hammer was watching the rock intently. He waited to make sure of its direction. Then he closed his fist over it again and stood up. He pointed to the southwest.

"That's the way," he said, and he started walking. Dhu got up to follow. The path by which he had come to Yellow Hammer's house did not run southwest, so Yellow Hammer led Dhu into the woods. In places the going was rough because of the thick undergrowth, but Yellow Hammer never changed his direction. He kept going straight ahead, due southwest. Dhu estimated they had walked about a half mile from the house when Yellow Hammer stopped. Again he dangled the rock on the string. Again he spoke to it, and again he watched it begin to swing. Then he started walking again, still toward the southwest. In another half mile or so he stopped and once again repeated the ritual, with the same results. Then he turned toward Dhu.

"This is unusual," he said. "Normally it will lead me in a circle, and somewhere in that circle will be the thing for which I'm looking. Normally it would have turned by now. Perhaps this is because we started from my house and not from where you lost this man."

"Does this mean that you can't help me?" asked Dhu.

"No," said Yellow Hammer. "It means that you must go southwest to find what you're looking for. Far southwest."

Dhu was puzzled. He wondered if Thane Savage and Bood Bradley were still in Texas. Perhaps instead of running north they had actually run farther south in Texas. He did not think that Thane Savage was that stupid, though. Texas was a big state, true enough, but a man wanted for murder in Texas could be arrested anywhere in Texas, and it might take a little while, but the word would get around. The smart thing to do would be to get out of the state.

He could have headed west, but it would take him a good while to get out of Texas going in that direction, and the same thing was true if he went east. But Yellow Hammer had said southwest. Well, Dhu thought, that could mean one of two things. Savage had gone deeper into Texas, like a fool; or, like a bigger fool, he had never left the general vicinity of Preston.

Well, he thought, there was one other thing. He knew that his friends back at the LWM would think that Yellow Hammer's ritual was a bunch of nonsense, nothing but hocus pocus. They would for sure think that Dhu had wasted his time with an old fool or a charlatan. His own teachers from the old Cherokee Nation schools would have said the same thing, and some of them had been Cherokee.

"The reason we have these schools," he had heard them say, "is to lift ourselves up from savagery into the light of civilization. We must save our people from the old superstitions." And there were times when Dhu had believed them, when he agreed with them. There had even been times when he himself had spouted that line. But he had discovered over the years that more often than not, when he was forced to think about these things, he did believe the old ways. But then perhaps he was just superstitious. He couldn't tell.

Anyway, it seemed that there was nothing for it but to go back to Texas and start over. Dhu decided that he would begin his return trip the next morning. But as he rode back toward Middle-striker's house he couldn't get the picture of the swinging rock out of his head.

Colbert rode down the lane that led into the LWM. He rode past the small cabin of Dhu Walker and on down to the main house. As he was dismounting there in front of the house Sam Ed noticed him from over at the corral.

"Howdy," he yelled.

Colbert looked in the direction of the voice and waved.

"How do," he said, and he started walking toward Sam Ed. They met about halfway between the house and the corral. Sam Ed held out his hand.

"You're Colbert, ain't you?" he said. "I ain't seen you for a spell. I'm Sam Ed Mc-Clellan."

Colbert's face wrinkled in puzzlement for a moment. Then its expression changed to a mild astonishment.

"Sam Ed," he said. "You the kid?"

"Well, yeah. I reckon," said Sam Ed. "Herd McClellan's my daddy."

"How is your daddy, son?" asked Colbert. "I heard about the shooting from Dhu Walker."

"He's getting better," said Sam Ed. "Boy, we was sure worried there for a while, but he's tough. He's pulling through."

"I'm sure glad to hear that," said Colbert. "Say, is Dhu Walker around?"

"No, he ain't. He went out after Thane Savage and Bood Bradley, the ones that done the shooting."

"I knew he was hunting them," said Colbert. "He come by my place a while back. But the reason I come looking for Dhu is that he asked me to watch out for them two and to let him know if I seen them. Well, I seen them."

"Savage and Bradley?" said Sam Ed. "Where? When?"

"Hold your horses, and I'll tell you," said Colbert. "They crossed the river on my ferry. Just this morning."

"Damn," said Sam Ed. "I wish I knew where to find Dhu. He's out there some-where looking for them."

"Slow down," said Colbert. "There's more. They was four of them."

"Four? Who was the other two?"

"I never got no names," said Colbert, "but they was four."

"Well, are you sure that two of them was Savage and Bradley?" asked Sam Ed.

"I'm as sure as I can be. Two of them

matched the descriptions Dhu give me, and the one was bossing the others around. And the clincher is that I heard the one that looked like the description of Bradley call the other one by his name. He called him Thane."

"By God," said Sam Ed. "It was them. And there's four of them now. Dhu needs to know that."

"Well, where's he at?" said Colbert.

"I don't know," said Sam Ed, and he was stomping around, nervous and agitated, raring to go, but he knew not where. "All's he said was that he was going after them two. He never said where he was going to look."

"Well, I done all I can," said Colbert. "I done what he asked me to do."

Colbert mounted his horse and rode out while Sam Ed stomped around some more. Finally Sam Ed stopped and stood still for a moment.

"I got to find Ben," he said.

Ben Lacey was in Preston on an errand when he ran into George McGee walking along the boardwalk.

"Howdy, Lacey," said McGee, but he gave no sign of pausing for conversation. He walked on by. Ben stopped, turned, and called out to the sheriff's back.

"McGee," he said.

The sheriff stopped and turned to face Ben. "Yeah?"

"You're spending a lot of time in Preston these days," said Ben.

"It's in my county," said McGee.

"I know, but we ain't seen a whole lot of you around here until just lately. What's up?"

"I'm still chasing after that damned Thane Savage," said McGee.

"Anything new?" asked Ben.

"I ain't sure. I came over here today because of a rumor that two cowboys has disappeared."

"Who was they?" asked Ben.

"Names're Arlie Puckett and Bill Yancey. As far as I know, I ain't never run into either one of them," said the sheriff. "Do you know them?"

"Yeah," said Ben. "Well, I don't really know them. I know who they are. They used to work over on the Colonel's spread south of here."

"That's where Savage worked, ain't it?"

"Yeah," said Ben. "It sure is."

"Well, I ain't sure what that means," said McGee, scratching his head. "Maybe nothing."

"Well, if I hear anything, I'll let you know," said Ben. He turned to walk across the street, but McGee stopped him.

"Lacey," said the sheriff.

"Yeah?"

"Where's your partner?"

"Dhu Walker?"

"Yeah. That one."

"I don't know," said Ben. "He went after Thane Savage. He didn't say which way he was going to look. He just rode out."

"If you hear anything about him, let me know that, too. You hear?"

"Sure," said Ben.

"Oh, yeah. How's old McClellan doing?" said McGee.

"Some better," said Ben. "I'll tell him you asked after him."

"Yeah," said McGee. "You do that for me."

Ben stood and watched as George McGee walked on down the street. Yancey and Puckett, he thought. He wondered if there might be some connection between their disappearance and Thane Savage's activities. He had no idea how those two got on with Savage. He couldn't recall having seen them together, but that didn't really mean anything either.

Maybe the disappearance of those two

cowboys didn't have anything to do with Thane Savage, but maybe it did, and if it did, Ben could think of only two possibilities. Either Savage had killed them, or they had joined up with Savage. Damn it, Ben thought, I wish I knew where to find Dhu.

Chapter

7

Almost three weeks had gone by since the day that Thane Savage had shot Herd McClellan. Dhu Walker was visibly dejected as he rode back onto the LWM property. He was tired and dirty. He had followed trails that had led him nowhere, and he had no idea where to look next. He stopped at his own cabin just inside the LWM property line, and he unsaddled his horse and turned it into the small corral there beside the cabin. Then he walked to the pump at the water trough. He worked the handle until the water came gushing out, and then he stuck his head underneath the stream. At first it was a shock, but then it began to feel good. For a while he just let it run over his head. Then he came up for air and brushed the wet hair back out of his face. He looked down the path toward the other two houses and thought about going on down to see everyone, but he decided against that for the time being. He would clean up first and change his clothes. Then he'd face them. He wasn't really eager to tell anybody that he had failed to accomplish anything on his mission, that he had found no trace of Thane Savage and Bood Bradley, that the last three weeks had been wasted.

Young Sam Ed McClellan was sitting on the porch of his father's house when he saw Dhu walking down the lane leading his horse. He jumped up and shouted toward the front door of the house.

"Ma, Dhu's coming."

Then he ran across to Ben's house and yelled again.

"Ben, Dhu's back. He's coming."

By the time Dhu reached the houses everyone was outside to meet him — everyone except Herd McClellan. Dhu stopped walking when he found himself surrounded.

"Where you been, Dhu?" asked Ben.

"Did you find them?" asked Sam Ed.

"Are you hungry, boy?" said Maude.

Dhu held up his hands for silence, and he got it. "Give me a chance here," he said. "I need to turn this old horse out."

"I'll take him for you, Dhu," said Sam Ed.

"Thanks."

Sam Ed took the horse and walked off,

leading him toward the barn and the main corral.

"Yes," said Dhu. "I'm hungry, and I sure would like a cup of good coffee."

"Come on in the house," said Maude, "You can tell us everything once you've et."

"Wait a minute," said Dhu. "First tell me how's Herd?"

"He's coming along real good," said Maude. "Come on in and see for yourself."

Inside Dhu went straight to the bedside of Herd McClellan. The old man was sitting up, propped against pillows. He smiled a broad smile when he saw Dhu.

"You look a lot more alive than when I last saw you," said Dhu.

"I don't even remember that time," said McClellan, "but I'm sure glad to see you now."

"Herd," said Dhu, looking not at the old man's face but at the quilt that covered the lower half of his body, "I haven't been able to find them. I haven't quit. I just came home to sort of regroup. Resupply. Get me a fresh horse. You know. I'll be going out after them again real soon, and —"

"Just hold on a minute," said McClellan. "You don't need to be going out nowhere.

I don't really recollect it, but it seems as how I sent you out after those bastards that shot me."

"Herd," said Maude, "watch your language in this house."

"Well, anyhow," said Herd, trying to ignore his wife's admonishment, "I don't recall it, but I guess I must have said it. I wasn't in my right mind, Dhu. Forget about them. Leave them to the law. We want you here with us, safe and sound. Manhunting's a lawman's job. It ain't yours, and I didn't have no right to ask it of you."

Dhu started to respond, but Maude spoke quickly, interrupting.

"Now you just come right on over here to the table and set yourself down," she said, taking Dhu by the arm. "I'll pour you a good, hot, fresh cup of coffee, and while you're sipping on that I'll heat up some beef stew and corn bread. You just relax."

She led Dhu to the table, and he sat down. Herd stayed in his bed, but everyone else followed Dhu and gathered around him once again. Mary Beth and Katharine followed Maude, offering to help, but Maude shooed them away.

"There ain't room in here for so many," she said. "Go on over there and set with Dhu."

"Now, then," said Ben, "where'd you go? What've you been doing all this time?"

Dhu sipped his coffee and put the cup back down on the table.

"Well, I followed Thane Savage's trail everywhere I could pick it up," he said, "but I always lost it. Then I went up to the Cherokee Nation and back. I figured that he'd run north. I never saw a sign of him, but I —"

Dhu paused. He thought about his visit to Yellow Hammer, and he knew that his white friends would never understand. They would simply think him superstitious.

"I got the idea that somehow I had gone north too soon, that they were still down this way. I think I went ahead of them or something. I don't know."

"Well, you were right about that," said Sam Ed.

"What?"

"Colbert come by here after you'd been gone several days," said Sam Ed, "and he told me that Savage had just crossed over the Red River into Indian territory on his ferry."

"I knew he'd go north," said Dhu, "and damn it, if I'd come back just now by way of Colbert's Crossing instead of the ford

82

farther east, I might have come across them along the way."

"And maybe you'd be dead," said Ben. "There's four of them now. At least that's what it seems."

Dhu glanced over at Ben.

"Oh, yeah?" he said.

"That's right," said Sam Ed. "Colbert told me that four men crossed over on his ferry."

"And in Preston," said Ben, "there's been talk about two cowboys, Arlie Puckett and Bill Yancey. They seem to have disappeared. Sheriff McGee thinks that they likely joined up with Savage and Bradley. It seems they used to work with them. Anyhow, they know each other."

"That sure does change the odds," said Dhu. "Savage, Bradley, Puckett, Yancey."

An hour or so later Dhu was sitting on the McClellan porch. He rolled a cigarette and lit it, and then he saw Katharine coming toward him from Ben's house. He stood up and waited while she walked across the way.

"Hello, Katharine," he said.

"Hello, Dhu. I'm glad you're back and safe."

"Thank you, but I'll be going out again."

"Even after what Herd said to you?"

"Even after that."

He took a long drag on his cigarette.

"Please sit down," said Katharine. "I didn't come over here to make you uncomfortable."

"No," said Dhu. "That's all right."

"Mind if I sit with you?"

"Okay."

They both sat, and for an awkward moment neither spoke.

"Why are you going out again?" asked Katharine.

"I don't know," said Dhu. "Because I said I would."

"But Herd —"

"I know what Herd said, but I also know what I said before that. I'm going after them, Katharine. I'll get them."

"But what if you don't get them?"

"I will. I'll keep looking until I do."

"Is it so important?" said Katharine. "Herd's going to be all right."

"I know that," said Dhu, "but they tried to kill him, and they almost did. And there's more to it than that. I don't know if I can explain it. Herd's my partner here. Mine and Ben's. When someone attacks my partner it's almost the same as if he'd attacked me. Does that make any sense to you?"

"I guess so," she said. "Some, anyway."

Dhu took a final drag of his cigarette and tossed away the butt.

"But there's something else still, isn't there?" said Katharine. "Some other reason you haven't told me about?"

Dhu looked at her, raising one eyebrow, his expression asking the question of her.

"Why," she said, "do I get the feeling that you're running away?"

"Running away?"

"From me."

Dhu leaned his forehead heavily on the heel of his palm. He looked down and away from Katharine.

"Katharine," he said, and the words came hard, but he knew that she had seen through him, right into his heart. He felt vulnerable, almost transparent. "It's true. I'm afraid of my feelings for you."

"Why afraid, Dhu? Are you afraid of how I'll return your feelings? Don't be. I —"

"No," he said, stopping her. "Don't say any more about it. Please."

"But I can't have you riding off into danger because of me," she said. "If anything happened to you, I'd never forgive myself."

"It's not you, Katharine," said Dhu. "It's me. That's all I can tell you. It's — it's all I can say."

★ ★ ★

It was early morning and still dark when Dhu saddled a fresh horse and tied on his bedroll behind the saddle. He left a note on the table inside his cabin. Ben or Sam Ed would go in looking for him and find it there. It was brief and to the point. He was gone again on the trail of Thane Savage. He was headed north. That was all.

By the time he reached Colbert's Crossing the sun was well up. Colbert ferried him and his horse across the river, and Dhu sat with him and drank coffee. Colbert gave Dhu a pretty good description of the four cowboys who had crossed on his ferry, so Dhu at last had descriptions and names. And finally he knew for sure that they had gone north. He had guessed right in the first place, but he had gone after them too fast. He thanked Colbert and tried to pay him for the ride.

"You know I don't take your money, Dhu Walker," said Colbert. "Now get on your way and good luck to you."

Dhu rode on. There was really no way to go except to follow the old Texas Road. He followed it for two days, and then he stopped at a roadside store. He tied his horse and went inside. The man behind the counter was an Indian. A Choctaw, thought Dhu. It was likely. He was in the Choctaw Nation.

Dhu picked up a few supplies and put them on the counter.

"Anything else?" asked the storekeeper.

"That's all," said Dhu.

The storekeeper added up the prices, and Dhu paid the bill.

"Just one other thing," he said. "I'm looking for four men. White men. They probably rode through here a while back."

"Lots of people come in here," said the Choctaw. "These four, they your friends?"

"No," said Dhu. "They tried to kill a friend of mine down in Texas."

The Indian storekeeper gave Dhu a questioning look through eyes that squinted almost closed.

"You from Texas?" he asked. "You look like Indian to me."

"I'm a Cherokee," said Dhu, "but I've got a ranch down there with two other men. My partners are white men."

"When you find these four men," said the Choctaw, "you going to kill them?"

"Unless they kill me first."

The Choctaw nodded his head.

"They was here, all right," he said. "Four white men. Looked like cowboys. They robbed me of all my money and some other stuff. Mostly food and bullets. They killed my clerk. He was just a young fellow, too. A nice Choctaw boy. They killed him."

"I'm sorry to hear that," said Dhu, "but I'm not surprised. These four are no good. Well, at least I know that I'm on the right trail."

"You on the right trail, all right," said the Choctaw. "If you see the Choctaw police, you tell them. They looking for those four, too. Maybe they got them by now. I hope so, anyway. If they don't, I hope you get them. Kill them all."

"I'll check with the Choctaw police," said Dhu. "Thanks."

As he continued on his way along the Texas Road Dhu Walker found himself hoping that the Choctaw police had not caught up with Thane Savage and his bunch. He wanted them himself. He wanted them badly. He wanted to kill them himself. This manhunt, he realized, had become an obsession with him.

Chapter

8

The wagon was fully loaded, and the load was covered up with a full sheet of canvas, tied down tightly at the sides. A man of about forty years was driving. He was dressed in a conservative business suit and wore a bowler atop his head. Beside him on the wagon seat was a young man, not much more than a boy. They were driving along the Texas Road headed north.

The driver pulled his wagon and team as far to the side of the road as he could when he heard the sound of several horses approaching fast from behind him. As he maneuvered the wagon and team he glanced over his shoulder to see four riders coming hard. They seemed to have no intention of slowing down, so he pulled back on his reins, bringing his team to a complete halt. The riders went on by, then stopped abruptly and turned to face the wagon and its occupants. They drew out their guns.

"Hey," said the wagon driver. "What is

this? What do you want?"

"Just get down out of that wagon," said Thane Savage. "Both of you."

"Who are you, and what do you want with us?" the driver demanded.

"I said climb down," said Savage.

Still the driver hesitated, and Thane Savage shot him in the chest. The body jerked backward, then flopped lifelessly forward, slumped over its own knees on the wagon bench. The young man jumped off the bench on the other side and ran. It was a short run into the thick brush and trees that grew along the roadside; even though four guns were firing after him, he managed his escape.

Bood Bradley dismounted and jerked the body down off the wagon. It landed in the dirt with a dull thud, and Bradley began going through the pockets of the man's suit. Thane Savage rode over close to the wagon and jerked the canvas cover off at one corner.

"What is it, Thane?" said Bradley.

"I don't know," said Savage. He rode around to the next corner of the wagon and pulled the cover off there, throwing it back as far as he could to reveal the contents of the wagon bed. Yancey rode over to get a look.

"It's hardware," said Yancey. "Tools and hardware. That's all."

"Shit," said Savage. "It ain't worth nothing to us." He turned to face Bradley, still squatted down beside the body of the driver. "What'd you find, Bood?" he demanded.

"Forty-seven dollars and thirty-five cents," said Bradley, "and a watch."

"And a bunch of shovels and bolts and such," grumbled Yancey.

"Shut up," said Savage. "Let's get the hell out of here." He lashed at his horse, continuing on his original northward course. The others followed him, all except Bood Bradley. Bradley, struggling to climb aboard a skittish horse, was left in their dust.

"Hey," he shouted. "Hold on there. Wait for me. God damn you. Wait a minute."

Just then the young man stepped out of the thicket. He hurried over to the wagon, unnoticed by Bradley, who had just managed to get a foot into a stirrup. The young man pulled a shovel out of the load of supplies, stepped around the wagon, and swung the shovel with all his strength. It thunked against the back of Bradley's skull with a sickening, deadly, dull sound. Bradley twitched and jerked foolishly, then dropped, his foot still caught in the stirrup.

The young man quickly tossed the shovel aside and scrambled for the six-gun at Bradley's side. The horse stamped nervously about, but the young man managed to get the gun before the horse started to run, south at first, then veering off the road to the west, dragging the lifeless Bood Bradley along by his foot.

All this had gone unnoticed by the other three riders, who had gotten a good head start by this time. A man with a rifle might have been able to get a good shot off at them, but it was too far for a handgun. Still the young man fired the revolver after them. At the first shot Savage and the others hesitated and looked back over their shoulders.

"Where the hell'd he come from?" said Yancey.

"Never mind," shouted Savage, and he kicked his horse and lashed at it with the reins, racing away. "Let's get out of here."

"What about Bood?" said Yancey.

"The hell with him," shouted Savage. "Come on." The three riders were soon out of sight, and the revolver was emptied of lead. The young man looked up the road and down, as if searching for someone to whom to appeal for help; then, seeing no one, he sank down on his knees beside the body of the driver. He took several deep breaths, and then he tossed the empty revolver aside. He looked at the body. The man was obviously dead. He stood up, ran again into the thicket, and disappeared.

Dhu figured that he'd reach the next town just about suppertime, and he liked that thought. He was tired of eating either his own camp cooking or cold trail food. He was hoping that there would be a decent eating establishment waiting for him up ahead in town. He hadn't seen any other travelers on the road for several hours, and so his mind had been wandering. He thought about food, but he had also found himself thinking often — too often, he told himself — about Katharine Lacey.

He was embarrassed that Katharine had seen through him so easily and so clearly. He had been uneasy around her lately, and it was obvious to Dhu that one of the reasons he was so anxious to go looking for Thane Savage was simply to get himself away from the LWM — and from Katharine.

And why did he want to get away from

Katharine? He was very fond of her. And she was a lovely and fascinating young woman. He had found himself interested in her right from the first time he had laid eyes on her back in Iowa, that time he and Ben had gone to get her from the Lacey family farm. And he had flattered himself that she was also interested in him. He was — in love? No. But that was what he was afraid of. He was afraid of his feelings for her.

At first it hadn't seemed that important. He had seen a beautiful young woman, and he had been interested. She seemed to return his interest, and that was kind of exciting. But then she had settled down with them at the LWM. She was not just Ben's sister then. She had become like a part of the whole LWM family, and Dhu had slowly come to realize that there was only one way in which he could manifest his interest in Katharine. He would have to propose marriage. Nothing else would work. It was all or nothing. Well, he wasn't ready for marriage. Yet he couldn't stand being around her and not expressing his interest in her.

He wondered just how long it would take him to chase down Thane Savage and his cronies. How long could he come up with

94

excuses to stay away? And if that was all he wanted — to stay away from the LWM — why did he not just leave, move back to the Cherokee Nation? That was his home. That was where he belonged. Not down in Texas living among white people.

Then he saw a wagon up ahead sitting beside the road. There didn't seem to be anyone in the wagon or anywhere near it. But as he rode closer he saw a body lying on the road beside the wagon. He urged his horse ahead a little faster. Getting closer to the wagon, Dhu pulled out his revolver. He looked around cautiously, but there didn't seem to be anyone around. It was quiet except for the stamping and breathing of his horse and occasional bird calls from the woods. He stopped beside the wagon, dismounted, looked around once more, then checked the body. The man was dead, all right — shot once in the chest. And not too long ago, it seemed. Dhu holstered his revolver and loaded the body into the wagon. He tied his own horse to the tailgate. Then he climbed onto the wagon seat, picked up the reins, gave them a flick, and started to drive.

Driving the wagon slowed him down quite a bit, and by the time Dhu reached the town the sun was low in the western sky. There were few people on the main street, and almost no businesses were open. He pulled the wagon up close to the board sidewalk, where he saw an Indian man walking along. The man was probably a Choctaw, so Dhu decided to try the white man's language.

"Hello," he said. "Do you speak English?"

The man stopped and turned to face Dhu. He appeared to be a full-blood.

"Not good," he said.

"Is there a lawman in town?"

"Lawman? Laws?"

"Yes," said Dhu, and he nodded his head toward the back of the wagon. The man looked back there and saw the body.

"I get 'em," he said, and he turned and ran off down the street. Dhu climbed down out of the wagon and secured it to the nearest hitching rail. Then he walked around to the back of the wagon and untied his own horse from the tailgate. He led his horse to the rail and tied it there. He looked down the street after the man who had gone for the law and saw no one coming, so he took the makings of a cigarette out of his pocket and rolled himself a smoke.

He lit the cigarette and took a long drag.

As he exhaled the smoke he saw the man coming back. There was another man with him. As the men came closer Dhu could see a badge on the vest of the second man. Dhu spoke first.

"You the law here?" he asked.

The Indian with the badge paused beside the wagon and looked at the body. Then he stepped toward Dhu.

"I'm Peter Tiger," he said. "I'm a captain with the Choctaw Lighthorse Police. Who are you?"

"My name's Dhu Walker. I'm from the Cherokee Nation originally, but I've been living on a ranch down in Texas. I was riding the Texas Road when I came across this. I thought I'd bring it on into town to report it."

"You just come across a wagon with a dead man in it?" said Tiger. "That's all?"

"That's all. The wagon was parked beside the road," said Dhu. "The body was on the ground beside it. There wasn't anyone else around, so I loaded him up to bring him in."

Tiger walked back to the back of the wagon and looked at the body again.

"He's been shot," he said.

"One time," said Dhu. "In the chest."

"And you didn't see anyone else on the road?"

"Not around there and not all the way in to here."

"Where you headed, Mr. Walker?"

"I don't know for sure. I'm trailing four men. One of them shot my partner in Texas and killed a bartender in Preston. I came across a storekeeper back down the road who told me that he'd been robbed by four men. He said they killed his clerk. Said you knew about it and you'd be looking for them. He gave me a description. They sound like the same men I'm looking for."

"You come across all kinds of things along the trail," said Tiger.

"Knowing those four are ahead of me," said Dhu, "I'm not surprised."

"Where are they now?" asked Tiger. "They haven't come through here."

"Then they must have left the road somewhere between here and where I found this wagon," said Dhu. "That is, if they did this, and I suspect that they did."

Tiger ducked his head and scratched the bridge of his nose.

"These men got names?" asked Tiger.

"The leader is named Thane Savage," said Dhu. "The three with him are Bood

98

Bradley, Arlie Puckett, and Bill Yancey. They're all cowboys."

"White?" said Tiger.

"All white."

"Walker," said Tiger, "I want you to stay in town tonight. In the morning I'd like for you to ride back out there with me. Show me just where you found this."

"All right," said Dhu. "Is there a hotel in town?"

Tiger jerked his chin toward the north end of the street.

"There's a rooming house just down there," he said. "Last house on the right. Just tell them the Lighthorse will pick up the bill. I'll come around for you first thing in the morning."

"Anyplace where I can get a meal?"

"Same place. They'll still be serving."

As Dhu settled down for the night in a comfortable bed he ran over the events of his trip in his mind. He knew that Thane Savage and his companions had started north on the Texas Road. He had gotten that information from Colbert, who had ferried them across the Red River. From there it only made sense that they would stick to the Texas Road. And then there was the robbery of the roadside store. The owner had given a description of the robbers and killers that had fit Savage and his gang. It just about had to have been them. And then there was the dead man at the wagon in the road. Again Dhu was almost certain that Thane Savage was responsible. But Tiger had asked the important question. If Savage and his gang had been ahead of Dhu on the road, and if they had committed the two murders, then where had they gone?

Chapter

9

After a good supper, a good night's sleep in a soft bed, and a hearty breakfast of ham and eggs and potatoes and gravy, Dhu Walker felt refreshed and ready to go. He was a little annoyed at having to go along with the Choctaw policeman, but he guessed that it couldn't be helped. He had just washed down his breakfast with a third cup of coffee when Tiger came in.

"Good morning, Mr. Walker," said the policeman. "Are you ready to go?"

"I'm ready," said Dhu. "I just have to go get my horse and get him saddled up."

"I've done that already," said Tiger. "He's right outside waiting for you. Let's go."

They rode out of town together heading south. For a while they rode in silence. Then Tiger spoke.

"You say you're a Cherokee?"

"That's right," said Dhu.

"But you've been living on a ranch down in Texas?"

"Yes. I told you that, too."

"You also said, I believe, that you were chasing four men who had attempted to murder your partner."

"Their leader, Thane Savage, shot my partner. He's apparently got three other men with him now. The ones I named for you."

"Yes," said Tiger. "You said your 'partner.'"

"That's right. I have two partners in a Texas ranch. The man they shot is named Herd McClellan. My other partner's name is Ben Lacey. We call the ranch the LWM."

"The LWM?" said Tiger. "I think I've heard of it. Lacey, Walker, and McClellan, is it? It's a pretty big spread from what I've heard."

"We're doing all right," said Dhu. He thought that he knew the question that was next in the mind of the Choctaw Lighthorseman. What's a Cherokee doing owning part of a Texas ranch? Dhu wondered what the answer to that question might be himself. Anyhow, Tiger didn't ask it.

"You planning to kill these men, Walker?" he asked instead.

"I'm thinking about it," said Dhu. "What are you planning to do if you catch up with them? You and I both know that you're not allowed to arrest white men."

Tiger's jaws tightened just a bit before he responded.

"That's right," he said, "but I don't intend to let them run loose killing folks around here. I can stop them — one way or the other."

"If you can find them."

"That's what you're along for," said Tiger. "To help me find them."

"Yeah, well, uh, if we run across them, and if they start to shoot, we'll just have to shoot back now, won't we?"

"Walker," said Tiger, "I've always believed that it was real foolish to just stand still and let a man shoot at you."

Dhu was getting anxious. He felt his blood begin to boil in anticipation of a fight. Thane Savage and his gang must be nearby. He was sure that they were responsible for the two killings along the Texas Road, and Tiger was just as sure that they had not passed through his town. Dhu felt like he and Tiger were headed for a direct confrontation with the outlaws. He hefted the revolver at his side to make sure it was loose in its holster. Then he saw a movement up ahead.

"What's that?" he said.

"It looked to me like someone came out

of those bushes," said Tiger, "then ducked back in when he saw us coming."

"Let's go," said Dhu.

"Hold it," said Tiger. "Be careful. Let's not rush into anything here."

He pulled a revolver out of his belt and nudged his horse forward. Dhu held back and did the same. In a couple of minutes they were at the spot in the road where they thought the man had gone into the bushes. They sat in their saddles, guns ready, looking around and listening.

"We know you're in there," said Tiger, raising his voice. "We saw you. Come on out. I'm Captain Tiger of the Lighthorse."

Dhu dismounted slowly and walked toward the thicket. Then he heard a rustling, and he stepped back, holding his revolver ready. His heart pounded. And then a young man stepped out into the road. Dhu guessed that he was maybe sixteen years old. He was dirty and ragged, and he appeared to be nearly exhausted. He was also obviously frightened. Dhu holstered his revolver, and Tiger shoved his own back into the waistband of his trousers and swung down out of his saddle. Holding out a hand, he stepped toward the young man.

"You okay, boy?" he asked.

"I'm all right," said the young man, but

he was gasping for breath. "You a law-man?"

"I'm a captain of the Choctaw Light-horse," said Tiger. "That's the state police of the Choctaw Nation. You're in the Choctaw Nation."

"Yeah, I know," said the young man. "They killed my boss."

"Was he driving a wagonload of hardware?" asked Tiger.

"Yeah. Four of them. They killed him, and I ran."

"All right now," said Tiger. "Just try to calm down and relax. Sit down here and catch your breath. Walker, bring him some water, will you?"

Tiger got the young man to sit down by the side of the road and lean back against a tree trunk while Dhu brought the canteen from his saddle. The boy took a long drink, Tiger took the canteen away from him to stop his guzzling.

"Slow down, boy. That's enough for now," he said. "You just relax a bit. Lean back there and take it easy."

"I'm all right," said the boy. "I need to tell about it."

"Then first," said Tiger, "tell me your name."

"I'm Jordy Blankenship. I work for —

well, I used to work for Mr. Howard Fast of Dallas, Texas. He owns — he owned Fast Implement Company down there."

"Was it Mr. Fast with you in the wagon?" asked Tiger.

"Yeah. We was bringing a load of supplies up here to a customer in McAlester. Mr. Porter. He's got a store in McAlester. Back there a ways, these four men come riding up behind us. Mr. Fast pulled over to let them get by, but once they went past us they turned and pulled out guns. They told us to get down, and then one of them shot Mr. Fast. I jumped and run. I been running and hiding out in the woods ever since. When I seen you coming I was scared it might be them come back after me. I think I killed one of them."

"How'd you do that?" asked Tiger.

"There was only the one body where I found the wagon," said Dhu.

"They had started to ride on, but one of them was kind of left behind. He was off his horse, kneeling down beside Mr. Fast. He'd been going through Mr. Fast's pockets. He was trying to get back on his horse, and I come out of the woods and grabbed a shovel from the wagon and banged him on the head. Then I got his gun and shot at the others, but I don't think I hit any of them. They was already too far off for pistol shots."

"What happened to the one you hit with the shovel?" said Tiger.

"He dropped right down like he was dead," said Jordy. "I think he's dead. Then his horse run off, dragging him along with it. His foot was caught in the stirrup. It caught when he fell."

"Which direction did the horse run?" said Dhu.

"Back south. Back that way." Jordy pointed down the road with a nod of his head. "That's the last I seen of him. I was too busy shooting at the others to watch him much."

"I was riding up from the south," said Dhu, "and I never saw him."

"Maybe he ran off the road somewhere," said Tiger. "Well, we've got another body somewhere, and we've got three outlaws running loose. We've also got a young man here who needs to be taken on into town and looked after."

"Oh, I'll be all right now," said Jordy. "You go on and do what you have to do. I sure do want you to catch those killers."

"Don't worry about that, son," said Tiger. "We'll catch them." He looked south down the road and wrinkled his brow. Then, "Walker," he said, "will you go look for that dead man and his horse while I take this boy back to town?"

"Sure," said Dhu. "I'm kind of anxious to find out who he is anyhow."

"You find them, load the body up, and head for town. I'll see you there or somewhere along the way. Come on, young fellow. Let's get you on my horse."

Dhu figured he'd been backtracking along the Texas Road for at least an hour and a half when he finally spotted the horse. It was standing off to the west or northwest in the middle of an open field. He could tell by its outline even from a distance that it was saddled, and when he got closer he could see the body, its foot still hung fast in the stirrup. The body had gotten tangled up in some low brush, and for that reason, apparently, the horse had stopped running. That was also the reason he stood still as Dhu approached.

The body was a mess, but Dhu, after untangling the foot, loaded it across the saddle. It was a mess, but he could tell that it was the remains of Bood Bradley. This was all the evidence he needed to confirm his previous strong suspicions. The two murders on the Texas Road had been committed by the Savage gang, and the remaining three killers could not be too far away. Taking Bradley's horse by the reins, Dhu mounted up and urged his own horse back toward the road.

Well, he thought, the odds have improved a little. Now there are only three. He didn't really care all that much about the others anyhow. They were just obstacles in the way. The one he really wanted was Thane Savage.

It was late evening by the time Dhu rode back into town leading the extra horse with its grisly burden. Captain Tiger had seen him coming and walked out into the street to meet him.

"I see you found them," said the captain.

"It's Bood Bradley," said Dhu, handing the reins to Tiger.

"Then you were right about the identity of the killers," said Tiger.

"Yeah. It sure looks that way. How's the kid doing?"

"He'll be all right. I had a doctor take a look at him. He was tired and hungry. Not hurt. Right now he's resting up over at the rooming house. I appreciate your help on this, Walker."

"Well, it's not over yet," said Dhu. "Say, I saw a road back there a ways going off to the east. Not much more than a lane, really. Where does it go?"

"No place much," said Tiger. "There's a small settlement out there. Just a few full-blood families. From there it goes on over into Arkansas. Wait a minute. Are you thinking —"

"The only thing I can think," said Dhu. "If you're right that they didn't come through here, and I didn't see them anywhere along the road —"

"Then they most likely moved off east on the only other road available to them, and they're headed for Arkansas right now," said Tiger.

Dhu put a foot in a stirrup and swung back up into his saddle.

"Where you going?" asked Tiger.

"I'm going after them."

"Well, wait just a minute," said Tiger. "It'll be dark soon, and they'll have to stop for the night. You'll have trouble out there after dark, too. That road's not much more than a cow trail in most places. Wait until morning, and we'll both ride out after them. We'll get an early start."

"What about those families out there?" said Dhu. "Aren't you worried about them?"

"They'll be all right," said Tiger. "Nobody comes down that road without them knowing about it, and when they see that it's white men coming, they'll just disappear."

"Even so," said Dhu, "I still don't know about hanging around here. Time's wasting. They've got a head start on me."

"On us, Walker," said Tiger. "Don't forget me. And listen, I know a shortcut from here. Wait until morning, ride with me, and we'll take it. It'll save several miles."

Dhu looked thoughtful but didn't respond.

"Go on, then," said Tiger. "But come morning you'll find that you're riding behind me."

"All right," said Dhu. "I'll wait, but make it early, okay?"

"I'll be rolling you out of bed, Walker," said the Lighthorseman. He turned and started to walk off down the street, leading the horse with the carcass of Bood Bradley slung across its saddle. Dhu sat in his own saddle and watched Tiger walk away. When the Choctaw turned a corner and vanished from his sight Dhu turned his horse around and started toward the rooming house at the other end of the street.

Chapter

10

It was mid-morning by the time Dhu Walker and Captain Tiger reached the road to Arkansas. They had taken the shortcut Tiger had suggested. When they reached the road they stopped and examined it for signs of recent travelers, and although they couldn't be absolutely sure, they agreed that it looked as if three men on horseback had passed by recently. By noon they reached the small full-blood Choctaw community Captain Tiger had mentioned earlier to Dhu.

"Wait here a minute," said Tiger.

Dhu hauled back on his reins, and Tiger rode up to the front of one of the small cabins while Dhu waited in the middle of the road. The front door of the cabin opened, and a woman appeared in the dark doorway. Tiger spoke to her.

Dhu could hear their voices, but not clearly. He thought, though, that he could hear enough to know that they were talking in Choctaw. In a few moments Tiger rode back to the side of Dhu.

"Come on," he said, and he urged his horse forward. Dhu moved along beside him. "They came through here, all right," said Tiger. "Three of them. They must have stopped back yonder somewhere for the night, because they're only about two hours ahead of us."

Dhu fought back an urge to lash his horse ahead, to hurry after them, but he knew better than that. As badly as he wanted to catch up with them, it wouldn't do any good to wear out his horse.

"I wonder how fast they're traveling," he said.

"I did, too," said Tiger, "so I asked. According to that woman back there, they're just sort of ambling along. She said they don't seem to be in any real kind of hurry. They must not think anyone's on their trail."

"Well, that's good," said Dhu. "Maybe we can catch up with them before dark."

"If we don't," said Tiger, "you're going to be on your own again."

"Oh? Why's that?"

"By dark they'll be across the border into Arkansas. I can't follow them over there."

Katharine Lacey had been unusually

quiet since Dhu had left the second time on his manhunt. She still helped Mary Beth with the baby, and she still did her share of cooking, dishwashing, and house-cleaning. But she didn't join in conversations enthusiastically as she had before. She didn't laugh much. And she seemed to use most of her spare time to get off somewhere by herself to sit and think.

She was leaning on the top rail of the corral staring off into space when Ben came riding in. A few feet away from her he swung down out of the saddle and tied the reins of his horse loosely around the rail. Then he walked over to stand beside his sister.

"How you doing, Sis?" he asked.

"Oh, I'm all right," she said, but the expression on her face remained listless.

"You sure?"

"Of course I'm sure. Why do you ask?"

"Well," said Ben, putting a foot up on the lower rail and scratching his head, "you just been awful quiet lately. You don't seem like yourself, you know? I thought something might be wrong."

She looked away.

"I don't know what you're talking about, Ben," she said.

"Well, suit yourself, but if there's anything wrong, I hope you'll tell me about it. We can still talk, can't we? I know I was out of your life while you were growing up, but I'm still your brother."

Ben walked back to his horse and unloosed the reins from the rail. Then he led the animal into the corral, unsaddled it, and turned it loose with a swat to its rump. The horse nickered, ran a few paces, then walked to the water trough. Ben walked into the barn with the saddle. A few moments later he reappeared. Katharine still stood in the same spot by the fence.

"Ben," she said.

"Yeah?"

"I'm sorry. You were right."

He walked back over to her, looking at her across the fence and leaning on the top rail. He waited for her to continue.

"It's Dhu," she said.

"What about him?"

"Ben, I think about him all the time. I can't help myself."

"Well, if you're worried about him," said Ben, "he can take care of himself. I've seen him in plenty of tough situations, and I know. But if you think I ought to go after him to help him out, I will. I don't know just where he is, but I guess I could find him, all right."

"No, it's not that. Not so much. I guess I am worried some about his safety. I know what he's doing is dangerous. But that's not really it. That's not all that's bothering me."

"Oh," said Ben. "I get it. I think. You're not — are you in love with him?"

Katharine waited for a long moment before she answered her brother's question.

"I guess I am, Ben," she said. "I just can't get him out of my mind."

Ben grinned, and he reached out and put a hand on Katharine's shoulder.

"That's okay," he said. "Dhu's a good guy. Oh, he's given me a hard time now and then ever since we knowed each other, but he's took care of me, too. Say, you're not worried because he's Indian, are you?"

"No," said Katharine. "Of course not. Nothing like that."

"I only just asked because it bothered me at first, but I guess I got over it all right. I don't mind it too much anymore. I don't even mind it that my sister's fallen for him. Anyhow, I don't think I do. It's okay, so cheer up."

"Ben, you don't understand. I'm not explaining myself very well. I think Dhu left because of me."

"What? No, he didn't. You know why he took off."

"I know he went after the men who shot Herd, but I mean — I think that he was anxious to get away because of me. I had a feeling even before Herd was shot that Dhu was wanting to get away. It seemed to me as if he'd been avoiding me lately. I thought he liked me, Ben, but lately —"

"Of course he likes you," said Ben. "I could tell that right away. I mean way back when he first met you. When me and him rode up to the farm to get you. In fact, it bothered me a little at first."

"I know all that, Ben. I saw it, too. At least I thought that I did. It's just lately that he seems to have changed. I can't explain it any more than that. I just feel it, that's all."

"Maybe you're wrong," said Ben, and he felt as he spoke that his answer was terribly inadequate. Damn Dhu Walker, he thought. He can make me feel stupid even when he's not around. "You know," he added, "Dhu's a hard one to figure sometimes."

"You know him better than anyone else. You're his best friend."

"Sis," said Ben, "I don't think anyone really knows Dhu Walker."

"Whoa," said Tiger, and he pulled back

on the reins of his horse, bringing it to a halt. The sun was already low in the west.

"What is it?" said Dhu.

Tiger pointed down and to his right.

"You see that rock over there?" he asked.

"Yeah."

"That marks the border. Over there's Arkansas. This is where I turn back. You going on?"

"I haven't caught them yet," said Dhu. "Yeah, I'm going on."

"Well, I think I'm just going to camp here for the night," said Tiger. "If I headed on back now, I'd be riding all night long. You want to join me?"

Dhu looked off into Arkansas, and then he looked at the sun.

"Sure," he said. "It is kind of late."

They were up early and ready to ride, but this time they would ride in opposite directions. Tiger climbed into the saddle first.

"Good luck, Walker," he said. "I wish I could go with you. When you catch those cowboys, will you be going back to Texas?"

"Yeah, I guess so," said Dhu.

"Do me a favor, if it's convenient. Will you?" asked the Choctaw.

"Sure."

"Stop back by and let me know how it all came out."

Dhu looked up at Tiger briefly and smiled.

"I will," he said. "Thanks, Captain." He nodded his head toward Arkansas. "What's the nearest town over there?"

"A little place called Hatfield. There's not much there. Well, so long."

"So long, Captain," said Dhu. He watched for a few minutes as the Choctaw policeman rode back northwest. Then he swung up onto the back of his horse and turned east.

It was almost noon when Dhu rode into Hatfield. Tiger had been right, he thought. There wasn't much to it. Two rows of buildings with false fronts facing each other gave the town a main street. Beyond that were a few scattered buildings, none impressive.

But the main street seemed to be almost too busy for the size of the town. Men on horseback rode up and down, and people crowded the sidewalks. Dhu found it a little puzzling, but he rode on into town. He had just gotten past the first building when two men with badges suddenly blocked his way. One held a shotgun. It wasn't pointed at Dhu, but it was menacing just the same.

"Hold on there," said the shotgun bearer.

Dhu looked down at the two men. Their faces were stern, almost mean. He moved his hands out away from his sides.

"You talking to me?" he said.

"I'm talking to you."

"You always greet strangers like this in Arkansas?" asked Dhu.

"Never mind that. What's your name, mister?"

"Dhu Walker."

"Where you from?"

"Texas. The LWM Ranch."

"You a cowboy?"

"I'm one of the owners," said Dhu. "I'm the W."

"Yeah? Well, what's your business here in Hatfield?"

"None at all. I'm just passing through," said Dhu. He was beginning to find the local law's line of questioning more than a little irritating. "What's this all about, anyway? You the sheriff here?"

"I'm the sheriff, all right," said the man with the shotgun, "and this here's my deputy. And we don't usually meet strangers this way, but our bank was just robbed, and a citizen killed, and we're just a little edgy around here over that."

"When?" asked Dhu.

"When was the bank robbed? Not more than an hour ago," said the sheriff. "I guess you can understand why we're watching strangers a little closer'n usual just now."

"It seems to me that it's a little late for that, Sheriff," said Dhu. "How many bank robbers were there?"

"There was three. Why you ask?"

"I'm trailing three men. They're wanted for murder in Texas and in the Choctaw Nation."

"You a lawman?"

"Nope. I'd be out of my jurisdiction if I was. They shot one of my partners down in Texas. I mean to get them if the law doesn't get them first. That's all. Oh, by the way, are you interested in their names?"

"Hell, yes," said the sheriff. "They're wanted for bank robbery and murder in Arkansas now."

"The leader's name is Thane Savage. The others are Arlie Puckett and Bill Yancey."

"Are you sure these that robbed our bank are the same three you're after from Texas?"

"I'm pretty damned sure. I've been right behind them on the trail," said Dhu. Then he gave the sheriff a description of Thane Savage. "I've never set eyes on his partners," he added.

"It's the same damn ones, all right," said the sheriff. "That description fits that one to a T. Well, all right, you can just come on along with us now, mister — what did you say your name was?"

"Walker," said Dhu. "Come on along where?"

"Posse's gathering over in front of my office. You're going to ride along with us, Walker. Let's go now."

Chapter

11

The Arkansas sheriff led a twenty-man posse out of town, heading north at a horse-killing speed. Dhu, bringing up the rear, did not try to keep up. If the bank had been robbed almost an hour before the posse left town, he reasoned, it would do no good to wear the horses out in the first two miles of hasty pursuit. It was not pleasant, though, eating the dust of the fools up ahead. He thought about dropping out and continuing on his own, or at least dropping even farther back. He told himself that if he did so, he would probably find himself a little later riding through the ranks of the worn-out posse and pursuing the Savage gang alone. Well, that would be just fine with him. That was the way he had started out. But then, he figured, there was just a slight chance that the posse might actually catch up with the outlaws, and Dhu did not intend to allow them to do that without him. He kept up with them just enough to keep eating their dust.

In a few more moments, though, the posse actually slowed its pace. Either the sheriff had come to his senses or someone up in the front ranks had warned him of the consequences of his foolhardy head-long rush. Dhu caught up with them and slowly worked his way up to the front, near the sheriff.

Then the outlaws' tracks suddenly veered off the road to the northwest, and the going became a little rougher. The posse reshaped itself into a long file with no more than two or three riders side by side.

"It looks to me like they're headed back across the border," said Dhu.

"Into the Indian Territory and out of my damned jurisdiction," said the sheriff. "God damn them all to hell anyway."

"Maybe we can catch them before they get there," said one of the other riders.

"Maybe," said the sheriff. Then he held up a hand and yelled out, "Hold on. Wait up here a minute."

He sat on his horse, leaning forward and off to his right, squinting down at the ground, which had become rough and rocky. Steep, rugged hills rose ominously not far ahead of them.

"What's wrong?" someone said. "Goddamnit," said the sheriff, "I've lost the trail." Dhu rode up slowly until he was beside the sheriff, but he didn't look down at the ground for the lost trail. He looked ahead. To their right the country was open, but to the left large rocks seemed to grow out of the ground. About a hundred yards ahead, still to the left, was a large clump of boulders. Just beyond the clump were the hills. Dhu looked at the boulders.

Frustrated, the sheriff climbed down out of his saddle to look more closely at the ground. Two more riders followed his lead.

"Damn it," said one of them, "there has to be tracks around here somewhere. The bastards couldn't have just up and disappeared."

"Hell," said the sheriff, "they went into them hills. That's where they went. They had to. There ain't no other place for them to go. And it's on the way to the border. The question is, did they turn hard left here, or did they ride on beyond them boulders up there? They had enough of a start on us to have did either one."

Just then Dhu saw a slight movement at the boulder cluster. He couldn't define it, but he knew that he had seen it.

"Watch out ahead," he said.

"What?" said the sheriff.

"Something or someone's moving around up there behind those rocks."

Then, almost as if to back up Dhu's statement, Bill Yancey popped up from behind the boulders and fired off three quick rifle shots. The first two went wild, kicking up dust and causing horses to jump and whinny and men to reach for their guns. The third struck a posseman who had been sitting in his saddle just behind Dhu and the sheriff and the other two dismounted men. The wounded man screamed in surprised pain and anger and grabbed for his left shoulder in a futile attempt to stanch the sudden flow of blood. He began to weave in his saddle.

Possemen climbed off their horses and began to fire wildly at the boulders ahead. Yancey dropped back down out of sight. The wounded man, trying to dismount, fell to the ground with a thud and a yell of pain.

"Hold your fire. Hold your fire," shouted the sheriff. "Goddamnit, you're just wasting ammunition. Don't shoot unless you got something to shoot at. Damn it."

There were a couple more shots following that admonishment, and then there was silence.

"What are we going to do?" someone

said in a harsh whisper.

"Well, shut up, and I'll tell you what we're going to do. First of all, stop looking at me. Keep your eyes on them rocks. That bastard might pop up and start shooting again any time, and I don't want no one else hurt if I can help it."

The sheriff looked over his shoulder at the men behind him and made a quick assessment of his situation.

"Now, Harley," he said.

"Yeah?"

"Get your horse and George's horse and lead them both back a ways out of range, and then you help George get back to town, and get him over to Doc's as fast as you can. George, can you follow him back there on your own?"

"I'll make it," said George. "Ow. Damn it all anyway. Shit. Why'd he have to hit me?"

"Aw, Merle," said Harley, "let someone else go. I don't want to miss the fight."

"Goddamnit, Harley, do as I say. I ain't got time to argue with you. Go on now."

"Shit," said Harley. "All right. Come on, George, Goddamnit. I'm going to miss all the fun. Why the hell couldn't you have ducked anyway?"

Harley grabbed the reins of two horses

and started walking back. George, clutching his bloody shoulder, followed along with a shuffling gait and a good many moans.

"Now," said the sheriff, "I want four men. Tom, Charley, Bennie, and you, Walker. You come along with us. You four and me, we're going to move out to our left. The farther we go, the longer his shot at us will be. When we get out there a ways we'll start toward him so that we'll come up at him from the side.

"The rest of you keep low and move up closer as you can. Keep him busy and keep him down, but don't waste ammunition. You hear me?"

"We got you, Merle," someone said.

"All right, then," said the sheriff. "Let's go."

He started running southwest at a crouch. Dhu and the others followed close behind him. As he ran Dhu kept glancing over his shoulder toward the boulders behind which Yancey was crouched. A few shots were fired by the other members of the posse as they moved forward.

Yancey raised himself again and fired. This time his shot was more effective. It dropped the nearest man in the main body of the posse. The others set up an immediate barrage, and Yancey dropped back down again. From his new position the sheriff looked back. He saw his man fall.

"Damn it to hell," he said. "Come on. Let's move."

From their position in the hills not too far away Thane Savage and Arlie Puckett could hear the gunshots behind them.

"They've caught up with Bill," said Puckett.

"Sure sounds that way," said Savage. "Well, he'll hold them there for a while."

He looked around, and his eyes stopped roaming when they came to the top of a rise just ahead and to his left.

"Arlie," he said, "why don't you ride around and get up on top there? If any of them gets past old Bill, you can pick them off easy from up there."

"No," said Puckett. "I ain't going to do that."

"Why the hell not? It's a good position. They'll have to ride right along here. Right where we're at. You can pick them off one at a time."

"Bill fell for that line, but I ain't," said Puckett. "I can tell from the shots back there that there's a whole bunch in that posse. Old Bill'll slow them down, all right, but he'll wind up dead. You want the same thing to happen to me."

"You think that's my plan? Hell, that ain't my plan. I don't know how many's in that posse, but old Bill's bound to kill a few of them. It won't be so big by the time it gets up here."

"I ain't staying back," said Puckett.

"Hell, all right," said Savage. "We better get to riding, then, before they catch up with us."

"If it'd be so damn easy to pick them off from up on that rise, why don't we both ride on up there and wait for them?" said Puckett. "Two of us up there could get them all a whole lot faster than one."

"Aw, forget it," said Savage. "Come on."

He lashed his horse and continued his way up the hill, still riding northwest. Puckett followed.

Dhu, the sheriff, and the three men with them were on their bellies. They had worked their way around until they were directly to the right of Yancey and could see him clearly. Yancey had been kept occupied by the other group and had not noticed their approach before, but then he saw them. It was a long shot, even for a rifle, but Yancey started shooting. His shots were off the mark.

"What do we do now, Merle?" said one of the men. "If we move up close enough for a shot, he'll have a better shot at us, too."

"And the other guys can't hit him now," said another. "He's well down behind them rocks."

"We'll just have to take a chance," said the sheriff. "Get your rifles ready, and let's inch closer."

"Wait a minute," said Dhu. "Let me try one."

"From here? It's a wasted shot."

Dhu, on his belly, put his rifle to his shoulder. His elbows rested on the ground. He took careful aim and slowly squeezed the trigger. There was a loud roar, and then, an instant later, a yelp of pain from Yancey. The outlaw seemed only to lean back against the boulders.

"By God," said the sheriff, "I think you hit the son of a bitch. Come on. Let's move in, but be careful. Watch him. He still might be able to shoot."

The sheriff stood up and started to run toward the boulders in a low crouch. Dhu and the others followed. They had gone about half the distance when Dhu saw Yancey slide down to a sitting position.

They ran on. When they reached the wounded outlaw they found him sitting on the ground, leaning back against the rocks, his rifle across his knees. The front of his shirt was covered with blood.

Yancey looked up at the five men who were suddenly gathered around him, all of them holding guns pointed at him. He was breathing heavily. He opened his mouth, and blood ran down his chin.

The sheriff reached down cautiously and picked the rifle out of Yancey's hands. He handed it back to another man, then got the revolver out of Yancey's belt and tucked it into his own waistband.

"Where's the other two?" he demanded.

But Yancey had stopped breathing.

"Damn," said the sheriff. "That was a hell of a shot."

He took off his hat and stepped around the boulder, waving at the other possemen.

"Come on up," he shouted. "Bring the horses. We got him."

Dhu was looking ahead into the hills.

In a few more minutes the whole posse was back together. Dhu got his horse and mounted up.

"Sheriff," said one of the men from the larger group, "Jimmy Dale's dead back there."

"Shit," said the sheriff. "Well, you and a couple of the boys take Jimmy Dale and this bastard here back into town. The rest of us will go after the other two. We ain't got no time to waste. They're headed for the border for sure."

As three men struggled to load up the dead outlaw the rest of the posse, now down to fourteen, mounted up. The sheriff, with Dhu right beside him, looked into the hills.

"Which way do you think, Walker?" he asked.

Dhu pointed almost straight ahead.

"That looks like the easiest way up and over," he said. "That's my guess."

"Let's go, then," said the sheriff, and he kicked his horse in the sides and started forward. Dhu stayed with him, and the others were right behind.

Chapter

12

Following the bloody encounter with Yancey, and because of the more rugged terrain on which they found themselves, the posse moved much more slowly than before, struggling more, exercising more caution, and watching every possible potential ambush site. Those who normally tended toward impatience thought back on the fallen Jimmy Dale and checked themselves a bit.

They found some more tracks when they got up into the hills a ways. Then they lost them again, but they had a pretty definite idea by that time where the two outlaws were headed and which route they were taking.

"They don't know this country," said Dhu. "They're just following the path of least resistance. Now that we know that, we can anticipate just about every move they're going to make."

"You think so, do you?" said Merle. "Well, I wish I could be as damned cocksure about it as you are. I'd feel a whole lot better about it if we was to find their goddam tracks again."

Dhu pointed toward the ground up ahead.

"Look over there," he said.

"Well, I'll be damned," said Merle. "You're right again. That's their trail for sure. Come on."

They kept riding, losing the trail again, finding it again, still moving northwest. They paused on top of a hill and looked around. They commanded a wide view in all directions, but the country was hilly and tree-covered.

"Anybody see anything out there?" said Merle, straining his own eyes.

"I can't see nothing but trees," said one of the men. "Trees, trees everywhere."

No one else could see them either.

"They could be anywhere out there," Merle said. Dhu pointed down a valley that ran north and west. "They're down in there," he said. "I'm just not sure how far along they are, how far ahead of us."

"Hell," said Merle, "you're probably right again. You been right about everything else up till now. Anyhow, I ain't got no better idea, so I reckon we'll just follow your instincts."

"Merle," whined a member of the posse, "I'm getting hungry. Ain't we ever going to stop and eat?"

"We didn't bring nothing to eat, you damn fool," said Merle.

"Well, what are we going to do? Damn. Look how low down the sun's getting. It's going to be dark before long. It's way past supper time."

Merle looked around, scratching his head.

"I don't know about the rest of you," said Dhu, "but I'm riding down there to the near end of that valley, and I'm going to make me a camp for the night. It looks to me like there's a stream down there."

"Camp out all night hungry?" whined the protester. "We might just as well give up and go home. By morning they'll be long gone anyhow. Hell, if I'd 'a' knowed it was going to be like this, I wouldn't have come. I ain't afraid of a fight, but I didn't know it was going to be like this. Shit. If we stay the night, they'll be long gone."

"They'll be stopping for the night, too," said Dhu. "Like I said before, they don't know this country."

"Turn on around and go home if you want to," said Merle. "Walker's right. I'm doing what he said. Anyone who's too chickenshit to go along with us, go on home. I'm tired of listening to your belly-aching anyhow. But you won't get there till midnight, and you might fall and break your goddam necks on the way trying to get through these hills in the dark."

There was a little more grumbling, but they all followed Dhu and the sheriff down the hill and into the valley. There was a stream there, all right, and they made camp by it. As the sun got lower a slight chill came into the night air, and they built a few small fires. Dhu unsaddled his horse. Then he dug into his saddlebags. He carried a small bundle over to Merle.

"There probably won't be enough of this to satisfy anyone by the time you pass it around," he said, "but it'll keep them from starving."

Merle took the bundle and gave Dhu a curious look.

"Hardtack and jerky," said Dhu. "Take it."

As Merle watched him Dhu took something else out of his saddlebags and walked over to the stream. Merle shrugged and started to distribute the food Dhu had given him. The possemen had not quite consumed it all when Dhu stood up and walked back from the stream dragging a string of fish. He dropped the string beside the nearest fire.

"Here's a little more," he said, "if someone wants to do the cleaning."

"By God, I will," exclaimed the one who had been whining and protesting just a few moments earlier. "I can clean a mess of fish slicker than snot. Damn, this is more like it. Merle, I sure am glad you brought this fellow along with us. I believe I'd have starved to death without him here. Him and his jerky and his fish. By God, you're all right, Walker."

They were up early the following morning and on the trail again, and they had only been riding for about an hour when they came across the signs of a camp. It was a trashy, negligent camp. The fire had apparently been left to burn itself out, and so it was difficult to tell just how long the campsite had been abandoned, but Dhu poked in the ashes for a few minutes and then stood up.

"I'd guess about an hour," he said.

"That means we ain't been gaining on them much," said Merle, "if at all. And damn it, in these hills I ain't going to know for sure whenever we cross over the border and get out of my jurisdiction."

They followed the trail a little farther, and then they lost it again. So, as Dhu had suggested earlier, they simply continued to take the path of least resistance. Then they saw a small cabin up ahead, a wisp of smoke rising up from its chimney.

As the riders pulled up in front of the cabin a dark round face peered suspiciously out of a window.

"Hello in there," shouted Merle. "Come on out. I'm the sheriff of Polk County, Arkansas. I want to talk to you."

The face in the window responded in a language that the sheriff did not understand, but Dhu Walker did. He swung down out of his saddle and stood for a moment beside his horse.

"Hold on a minute, Sheriff," he said. "Let me talk to him."

Dhu took a step toward the window.

"'Siyo," he said. *"Tohiju. Ayuh Inoli Edohi."*

The other answered him, and the sheriff looked back at the posse and shrugged as a brief conversation took place at the window.

"I'm damned if I know what the hell they're saying," he said.

In another moment Dhu walked back to his horse. He turned once more toward the window. *"Wado,"* he said. Then he put a foot in the stirrup and grabbed the saddlehorn.

"Now just what the hell was all that?" said Merle.

"Cherokee," said Dhu, pulling himself up onto his horse's back.

"What?"

"We're not only out of your jurisdiction, we're farther north than even I thought we'd gone. We're in the Cherokee Nation. Anyhow, Savage and Puckett rode by here about an hour ago. They're likely headed back toward the Texas Road."

"Damn," said Merle. "Well, then, Walker, I reckon right here's where we part company. I got to take these men back home. There's nothing left for me to do but only to just notify the U.S. Marshal's office. That's all I can do. They can chase them in there. I can't."

"Neither can the Cherokee law," said Dhu. "No one can except the federal marshals. And me. It's been a pleasure, Sheriff."

Dhu touched his hat and flicked his reins and rode on ahead alone. Merle sat slouched in his saddle and watched Dhu for a long moment.

"Well, I'll be a son of a bitch," he said.

"Say, boys. What do you want to bet he catches those bastards?"

"Merle," said one, "is he a damned Indian?" Merle jerked the reins on his mount to turn it around.

"Come on," he said. "Let's go home."

"Thane," said Puckett, "do you know where the hell we're at?"

"No, I don't," said Savage. "Not exactly. But I think that we're out of Arkansas. I think that posse had to turn back. We must be back in Indian Territory again by now. That's what I think."

"Them Indian police will be after us again, then."

"I ain't sure. Them was Choctaws. The Indian territory ain't all the same. They's Choctaws and Creeks and some others. I don't know what all. We'll have to find out whether we're in the Choctaw Nation or one of them others. That's all."

"Too bad that old son of a bitch back yonder in that cabin couldn't talk American," said Puckett. "He might could've told us."

"I should have killed him," said Savage, "but I wasn't sure yet that the posse had stopped, and I didn't want to take a chance on them hearing no shots."

Puckett suddenly reached over and put a hand on Savage's shoulder.

"Listen," he said. "You hear a wagon?"

They sat quiet and still for a few seconds.

"Yeah," said Savage. "Sounds like it. Come on."

They rushed ahead through brush grown up as high as the tops of their boots on horseback, and then they saw the road. The sounds of the approaching wagon became louder, and then the wagon came into view. As it drew nearer they shouted.

"Hey, hold up there a minute, friend."

The driver of the wagon pulled back on his reins, but as the wagon came to a stop he reached down and picked up a shotgun. He didn't point it directly at the two strangers, but he held it ready.

"Hey," said Savage, "there ain't no need for that scattergun. We're just a couple of lost Texas cowboys wanting some information. You live around these parts?"

"Not far," said the driver.

"Well, just where in blazes are we at?"

"You're in the Cherokee Nation. The Sequoyah District. Just west of the Arkansas line. You say you're from Texas?"

"That's right," said Savage.

"Well, if it's any of my business, how'd you boys get lost up here?"

142

"We rode north looking for work. You know about any jobs to be had around here?"

"Not for cowboys," said the driver. "You'll have to go farther north and west. Up in Cooweescoowee District. Or over in the Outlet."

"Oh. Okay. We'll try that. Thanks, partner."

"Sure."

The driver sat and waited for the two cowboys to move on. He wasn't about to put down his shotgun to drive off.

"Say," said Savage, "I'm curious about something."

"What's that?"

"You look like a white man to me, but you said you live around here. You live over in Arkansas?"

"I live here," said the driver. "I'm a Cherokee citizen, but I'm three-fourths white."

"Oh."

"You boys riding on up north, then?"

"Yeah. I guess we will. What's the best way for us to get there?"

"The Texas Road. Take this road here, and go back the way I just came. It'll take you right to the Texas Road."

"How far?"

"You'll be there by dark."

"That long, huh?"

" 'Bout that long."

Savage looked at the shotgun for a moment. He had money in his pockets from the bank robbery, and he wasn't wanted yet in the Cherokee Nation. He smiled and touched his hat.

"Well, thank you, friend," he said. "I guess we'll be headed for the Texas Road. Come on, Arlie."

The driver of the wagon held his shotgun and watched over his shoulder until he was sure that the two were well on their way. Then he put the gun down, picked up the reins, and went on his way.

It was less than an hour later when Dhu Walker got down off his horse to examine the hoof marks there beside the road. His eyes followed them out into the road, where they crossed the tracks of wagon wheels and turned west. The wagon tracks continued east. It looked to Dhu as if the two outlaws had paused there for a spell. So had the wagon. Then the outlaws had gone their way, and the wagon had gone its way. He hoped that all was well with the occupants of the wagon. Then he moved out, following the tracks of the outlaws' horses.

Chapter

13

"It sure as hell don't look like much of a fort to me," said Arlie Puckett. "What the hell kind of a fort is it, anyway?"

"A fort's a fort," said Thane Savage. "Don't you see them goddamn blue-bellies down there?"

"There ain't very many of them."

"Well, I guess it ain't a big fort, but it's a fort just the same. And besides that, any blue-bellies is too damn many Yankees for my taste."

Savage kicked his horse in the sides and started it down the hill toward Fort Gibson.

"We going on down there amongst them soldiers?" said Puckett.

"They don't know us," said Savage. "And they likely got a store down there anyhow, and a place to eat, maybe. Come on and don't worry. If anybody asks, we're just a couple of out-of-work Texas cowboys looking for a job. You got it?"

"Sure," said Puckett. "I got it. Say, you reckon they got any whiskey down there?"

"You keep your mouth shut about whiskey, you dumb ass," said Savage. "Don't you remember nothing for more than five minutes? We're in Indian Territory again. We ain't in Arkansas no more. Whiskey's against the law in Indian Territory. You go asking around a army fort in Indian Territory for whiskey, and you're liable to get us throwed in jail."

"I forgot, all right? I won't say nothing about it while we're in the fort."

They rode a little farther in silence, and then Puckett spoke up again.

"Thane?"

"What?"

"Ain't Indian Territory in the United States?"

"I don't know for sure," said Savage. "I don't think so. Not exactly, anyhow. Just sort of, I guess."

"Well, I don't see how it could be, if whiskey ain't legal."

They rode on down the hill and into the fort. There were a few log buildings, and there was yet part of a wall. As Arlie Puckett had said, it didn't look like much of a fort. Scattered log houses could be seen here and there in the distance. Fort

Gibson had more the look of the center of a community than an army post. There were soldiers — not a great many of them, but they were there.

And the fort was busy for such a small place. The civilian population was bustling about. It was made up of both Indians and whites, or at least people who appeared to be white. Savage and Puckett had learned already that there were numerous mixed-blood citizens of the Indian nations who looked like whites.

Savage and Puckett at first just sat on their horses looking around, watching the people come and go. They noticed a public eating house and an administrative office. They also located the store.

"Let's go over there and see if we can't find ourselves a steak dinner," said Savage.

They rode over to the eating house, dismounted, and tied their horses to the hitching rail outside. They looked around a little more, then went in. The small place was crowded and busy, but they did manage to get themselves a table against the far wall, and eventually a woman approached them.

"What can I get for you?" she asked.

"Steak," said Savage, "if you got it."

"We got it," she said. "Both of you?"

"Yeah," said Puckett.

"Coming up."

"And coffee," said Savage.

The woman walked away, and Savage reared back in his chair to survey the room. The crowd was like that outside. It was a mixed crowd of Indians, soldiers, and civilians who might be mixed-blood Indians or white. Savage was about to settle back down to talk to Puckett when he caught himself looking directly into the eyes of a man at the table next to his own.

The man gave him a hard look back. He was seated with two other men, all three with the look of border hardcases. Savage was initially embarrassed to have been caught staring at the man, but he recovered quickly.

"Uh, excuse me, there," he said, "but me and my pal here, we're strangers in these parts, and, uh, you look like white men to me. Am I right?"

"You goddamn right," said the man. "I'm pure-dee white through and through."

"Good," said Savage. "I thought so, but I been fooled before in this Indian Territory. Say, what the hell kind of a fort is this anyhow?"

"Ain't much of a one anymore," said the

man. "Mostly it's a Indian agency now —
for the Cherokees. That's about all."

"Oh," said Savage. "I see. Well, that's
just fine, I guess. Hell, I was about half
afraid that we was going to run into a
whole damn fort full of goddamn Yankee
blue-bellies down here."

"You a rebel?" asked the man.

"Damn right," said Savage. "Me and my
buddy here both. We're just up from
Texas."

"We got room over here," said the man.
"You and your friend pull your chairs on
over, if you've a mind to."

Savage and Puckett got up, dragged their
chairs over to the other table, and sat down
again.

"I'm Thane Savage, and this here is
Arlie Puckett."

"I'm Charlie Summers," said the other,
and then he pointed to his two companions. "Skeeter and Red Jack. What'd you
say your business was?"

"I don't remember saying," said Savage,
"but we're cowboys. Out of work just now.
What about you?"

"We're businessmen," said Summers.

"And we just been put out of business,"
said Skeeter.

"Shut up," said Summers.

"Here comes our food," said Red Jack. "Let's eat."

Dhu followed the tracks of Thane Savage and Arlie Puckett back to the Texas Road, and he was pretty sure that they took the road headed northeast. But almost as soon as he made the turn he lost the tracks. The Texas Road was well traveled. So there was nothing to do but follow the road. He knew that he had been at least an hour behind them for some time, so he hurried his horse as much as he dared. He hoped to catch up with them before they left the Cherokee Nation or before they did anything to harm any Cherokee citizens. Fort Gibson was not far ahead. Maybe they had stopped there.

About an hour later Savage and Puckett found themselves at a secluded campsite on the banks of the Grand River with their three newfound friends. Summers had produced a jug of whiskey from some secret hiding place, and the five men were sitting in a circle around a small fire and passing the jug.

"So what's your business?" asked Savage. "If it's any of my business." He laughed out loud at his own feeble joke.

Summers waited for Savage to stop laughing. Just then Skeeter, sitting to the left of Savage, passed Savage the jug. Savage took it and tipped it up to his lips, tilting his head way back.

"You're sucking on it," said Summers.

Savage swallowed and gave Summers a long, hard look.

"Whiskey?" he said. "You sell whiskey? In the Indian Territory? Ain't that just a bit dangerous?"

"It's getting to be," said Summers. "Fact is, we was just told to get the hell out of the nations and never come back."

"Who told you that? Ain't this a free country?"

"The United States Army told me that," said Summers. "They seem to suspect me of breaking the law, but they ain't got proof enough to throw me in jail. So they told me to get out."

"Those dirty blue-belly bastards," said Savage. "They think that wearing that goddamn little blue suit makes them gods or something."

"Well, they're the law in these parts. Them and the federal marshals."

"I thought the Indians had their own laws," said Savage.

"They do," said Summers, "but they can't arrest white folks. But the U.S. can, and they do, too, if they can catch you."

"That ain't hardly fair," said Savage. "Making a man look out for all different kinds of laws at the same time."

"It ain't fair, but that's the way it is."

"So what are you going to do now?"

"I ain't decided."

The jug had just reached Summers again, and he took a swig.

"There's other ways of making a living," said Savage.

Summers passed the jug along and smiled back at Savage.

"Punching cows?" he said.

Savage gave a sly look to Puckett, and he reached inside his coat to pull out a handful of bills. He held the bills up for Summers and the others to see. Summers's eyes opened a little wider.

"You never made that punching cows," he said.

Savage tucked the money back inside his coat.

"We, uh," he said, "we kind of went into the banking business here lately. Me and Arlie here. We kind of been looking for some good men who might be interested in joining up with us."

★ ★ ★

Dhu rode into Fort Gibson at sundown. People were still milling about, but most of the crowd had vanished, most of the bustle had ceased. He went to the administrative office but found it closed for the day, so he rode over to the public eating house and went inside.

There were yet a few other late customers in the place. Dhu found himself a table and chair and sat down. A man wearing a greasy apron came over to the table.

"What'll you have, stranger?" he asked.

"What have you got left to eat this late in the day?" asked Dhu.

"I can fry you up a steak, or else I've got some good beef stew left."

"You have corn bread to go with that stew?"

"Yep. And butter."

"Stew and corn bread, then," said Dhu, "and coffee."

He rolled and smoked a cigarette while he waited for the man to bring his food. When the man brought it Dhu asked for more coffee. He tasted the stew while the man was going back for the coffeepot. It was hot, and it was good. The man came back and was pouring Dhu some more coffee.

"The stew's good," said Dhu.

"Thanks."

"You see a couple of strangers around here earlier today?"

"Mister, there's crowds of people in and out of here every day. They're all strangers to me."

"Many Texas cowboys?"

The man looked at Dhu for a moment, then walked away and went back behind his counter. Dhu finished his meal and went to the counter to pay. He put his money down and started to leave.

"Mister," said the man behind the counter.

Dhu turned back to face the man again.

"There was two cowboys in here today. I noticed them because they was real fancy dressers, you know? Wide hats, tall boots, like — well, no offense — kind of like you."

"How long ago?" asked Dhu.

"I'd say three, four hours."

"Damn," said Dhu. If the man had seen Savage and Puckett, he was farther behind than he had thought. "You wouldn't know if they're still around, would you?"

"Wouldn't know about that, but I'll tell you one more thing. They left here with three other men. And I know them three. Charlie Summers and Skeeter and Red

Jack. That's all the names they got. Skeeter and Red Jack. They're whiskey peddlers. I heard the army run them off today and told them not to come back. Them two cowboys I seen, they left with Summers and Skeeter and Red Jack. I don't know where they went."

Dhu put a bill on the counter in addition to the change he already left.

"Thanks," he said.

He stepped outside. The sun was about to disappear behind the trees. It would be dark soon, and there was no sense in trying to search further until morning. Again he figured that Savage and the others would be stopped somewhere for the night, so at least he wouldn't be falling any farther behind by stopping. He was also wondering what the post commander might be able to tell him about these three whiskey peddlers.

And just because two cowboys who might be Savage and Puckett had been seen to leave the eating place in the company of the whiskey peddlers didn't mean that they had left Fort Gibson in that same company. He wanted to talk to more people around the fort and try to confirm the identity of the two cowboys. He also wanted to find out if anyone had seen them leave, either alone or in other company. And if the evidence all seemed to continue to point to the probability of Savage and Puckett having been joined by these other three, he wanted to find out what he could about these new ones: Charlie Summers and Skeeter and Red Jack. He repeated the names in his mind so that he wouldn't forget. Then he went to find a place to board his horse and another where he might sleep for the night.

Chapter

14

Dhu was up early. He had his breakfast, then saddled and packed his horse. Taking the reins, he led the horse, walking toward the administrative office. It was a small cabin that stood by itself in the middle of the fort area. He tied his horse to the hitch rail in front of the office and was about to go in when the door opened and a young officer stepped out the door. Dhu recognized the captain's bars on the uniform.

"Excuse me, Captain," he said. "Have you got a minute?"

The soldier stopped and looked at Dhu.

"Yes, sir," he said, extending his right hand. "Captain Rollins. How can I help you?"

Dhu took the man's hand.

"I'm Dhu Walker. I came up from Texas trailing four men. Two of them were wanted for murder and attempted murder in Texas. I followed them through the

Choctaw Nation and into Arkansas. Along the way they killed a man in the Choctaw Nation while robbing a store, and another one they robbed on the road. In Arkansas they robbed a bank and killed a man. Two of them were killed along the way, so now they're down to two. The only thing is, I think they may have joined up with three more right here last night."

"Have these men got names, Walker?"

"The two survivors from Texas are Thane Savage and Arlie Puckett. I think they joined up with Charlie Summers, Skeeter, and Red Jack."

"We ran those three out of here yesterday," said Rollins. "They're whiskey runners. There's no doubt about that, but we couldn't prove it on them. So we ran them out as undesirables. We can do that in the territory, you know."

"Yeah, that's what I heard."

"Are you a lawman, Walker?"

"Nope."

"Then what's your interest in this matter?"

"One of the men they shot is a partner of mine. I promised him that I'd get them."

"I really should tell you that you ought to leave it up to the law."

"Yeah," said Dhu. "Which law?"

"You never answered my original question."

"Sorry. I guess I forgot it."

"What can I do for you?"

"Oh, yeah. Well, can you tell me anything about this Summers and his buddies? Where are they from? Where might they be going? Anything."

"They come out of Arkansas, as far as I know," said the captain. "They're mean and tough, but not very bright. Summers is the smartest of the three. That's not saying much. My guess is that they headed back for Arkansas."

"That wouldn't be very smart of Savage and Puckett, though," said Dhu. "They're wanted for murder and bank robbery in Arkansas."

"I wouldn't know about that. We can ask around and try to confirm the information you got — that they all left here together."

"I'd appreciate that," said Dhu.

Dhu accompanied the captain around the fort. Now and then the captain stopped someone to interview him. Some were soldiers, some civilians. Most didn't know anything about the two cowboys, but one who had still been hanging around the fort in the late afternoon of the previous day had seen them.

"They all left here together," he said. "I seen them."

"Did you see which way they went?" asked Dhu.

"Sure. They headed for Summers's camp."

The captain took the man by his arm and led him to the stables, where he ordered two horses to be saddled. Dhu mounted his own horse, the captain and his informant the two from the stable.

"Take us there," said the captain.

It didn't take long to ride to the campsite on the river, but no one was there. Dhu was the first one off his horse and looking around. He found the empty jug, and he kicked it in frustration.

"Damn," he said. "They were right here while I was at the fort. They had to be."

Captain Rollins walked around, casually looking at the ground.

"Walker," he said, "take a look at this."

Dhu walked over to join Rollins.

"What is it?" he asked.

"Look at that print. Looks like a corner was filed off that horseshoe."

"Yeah. That's pretty distinctive."

"That shoe is on Summers's horse. Well, it looks like they're gone, and there are no warrants out for any of them in the Cherokee Nation. If there are federal warrants, I haven't seen or heard of them yet. Is there anything more I can do for you?"

"I guess not," said Dhu. "I think I'd better get on their trail. Thanks for your help, Captain."

Dhu left the captain and the informant and rode back out of the fort and onto the Texas Road once again. The peculiar track made by the horse of Charlie Summers made it much easier to stay on the trail of his quarry, and when they left the Texas Road and headed north toward Kansas Dhu had no trouble telling it. He didn't have to stop to study the tracks. He just followed them. They were clear.

And he figured that the information he had gotten from the fort was correct, for he was following five horsemen. Almost for sure that meant Thane Savage, Arlie Puckett, and their three new companions, Summers, Skeeter, and Red Jack.

The biggest problem was that once again Dhu had no idea how far behind he was. But still he followed the distinctive track. He followed it to the northern boundary of the Cherokee Nation and into the state of Kansas, to Baxter Springs and to Fort Scott. It was in Lawrence that he at last caught up. He found the horse with the distinctive track.

It was in a livery stable. Dhu found the stableman and cornered him. He pointed out the horse.

"Who owns that one?" he demanded.

"Why, I do," said the stableman.

"Since when?"

"Yesterday afternoon. I've got a bill of sale."

"I don't care about that," said Dhu. "Just tell me who you got it from and where I can find him."

"Sure. I got it from Karl Ackerman. He's got a farm west of town."

Dhu found the Ackerman farm all right, but he was worried. Something had gone wrong somewhere, and again he was losing valuable time. Mrs. Ackerman was at the house. She told Dhu that he'd find Ackerman out behind the barn. He was working on a holding pen. Dhu thanked her and walked around behind the big red barn.

"Karl Ackerman?"

"That's me. Who's wanting to know?"

"My name's Dhu Walker, Mr. Ackerman. I just came from the livery stable in town. The man told me that he bought a horse from you yesterday afternoon. That right?"

"That's right. Anything wrong with it?"

"Not that I know of," said Dhu. "It's just that I've been trailing that horse for a good long while. Would you mind telling me where and when you acquired it?"

"No, I don't mind. I bought him off a fellow in Fort Scott four days ago."

"In Fort Scott," Dhu repeated. It was not a question. It was just a repetition. Dhu chastised himself silently. Four days ago. For the last four days he had been following Karl Ackerman to Lawrence. Damn it.

"If it will help you any," said Ackerman, "the fellow was with four others. They wanted to sell all of their five horses, but the one was all I bought. I wish I'd had more money, though. I'd 'a' took them all. Their prices was right. They said they needed the money for railroad tickets. Said they was going north."

Back at Fort Scott Dhu found the railroad station. He questioned the man behind the counter, but the man couldn't remember any specific customers from over a week ago. But he did show Dhu the train schedule for that day, the day that Ackerman had bought the horse, and for the next day. There was only one place to go on the one track going north out of Fort Scott, and that was Kansas City.

Where would they go from there without horses? Dhu wondered. They had sold their horses at Fort Scott. Of course, they could get more horses at Kansas City. They sold their horses cheap, according to Ackerman, but then Savage and Puckett might have plenty of the bank money left yet. And even without the bank money they could simply steal more horses when they needed them. They were, after all, thieves.

Dhu bought passage for both himself and his horse to Kansas City. There was nothing else to do.

So he found himself in Kansas City. He was at least a week behind Savage and the others. They could have gone in any direction out of Kansas City, but Dhu eliminated south as a possibility right away. They had been moving north. He didn't think that east was a very real possibility either. Savage and his gang, Dhu thought, would go north or west. And furthermore, he reasoned, they would go somewhere there was something to steal.

The railroad didn't go any farther north. In fact, Kansas City was a dead end for the rails unless one wanted to go east. They had probably bought some more horses and ridden out north or west — or northwest. Of course, they could have stolen some horses, but he doubted that. There were too many law officers in Kansas City, too much danger of apprehension. Dhu didn't know Summers and the other two former whiskey runners, but from what he knew of Thane Savage, he didn't expect them to take any chances.

Without straying too far away from the railroad depot Dhu started checking for stables and any other places horses might be bought and sold. He had been in the city two days when he came across a wagon yard. In the back was a small corral. In the corral were a few horses.

"Those horses back there for sale?" asked Dhu.

"Yep."

Dhu rode back to the corral and looked the animals over. The man followed him.

"They don't look like much," said Dhu.

"They ain't much," said the man. "I had some better, but I sold five all at once about a week ago. I ain't had no new ones in since then."

"Five at once?" said Dhu.

"That's right."

"All to one man?"

"Nope. They was five of them."

"Well, I'll be," said Dhu. "That's something, I guess. I bet that's kind of unusual in your business. What were they? Local ranchers, I bet."

"Nope. You're wrong about that. I never seen them before. I don't know everyone in these parts, but I could tell these men wasn't local. They talked funny, you know. I got a good ear for that sort of thing. They was from down south. Arkansas. Texas maybe."

"I don't suppose you know which way these men headed when they left here," said Dhu.

"Nope. Ain't got no idea. And you ain't fooling me none either, young feller. You never was interested in my horses. You're tracking them five men, ain't you?"

Dhu took off his hat and scratched his head. He grinned down at the old man from up in his saddle.

"Well, now," he said, "you sure got me there. I guess nobody ever puts much over on you."

"That's for sure."

"Well, thanks for your time."

"Don't you want to know what kind of horses they rode out on?"

"Well, yeah. Sure," said Dhu.

"All right, then, I'll tell you. They was a black stallion with three white stockings. They was a gray mare, kind of small, she is. A roan stallion. A buckskin gelding. And the last was a paint pony. Pretty little thing. I kind of hated to let her go, but they paid good money. Didn't argue or nothing."

"That sounds like the men I'm after," said Dhu.

"They rob a bank or something?"

"Yeah. Among other things."

So they had five new horses, and Dhu had descriptions of the horses. He'd be able to spot them from a good distance away. He would also be able to more easily describe them to others. But what would he do next? Just ride circles around Kansas City looking for the tracks of five horses? That didn't make much sense.

It was late afternoon, and places around the city would soon be closing for the day. As badly as he wanted to get back on the trail, Dhu decided that he'd spend one more night in Kansas City. In the morning he would check out the stage routes. Savage and his gang wouldn't ride out on a stage, but they would want to head in the direction of some kind of civilization.

They'd been spending money like rich men. They were likely running low, and they'd be looking for a small town with a bank.

Chapter

15

The cold struck hard and fast, sudden and unexpected, and the five riders from down south were shocked, surprised, and scared.

"How far are we yet from the next town?" said Skeeter.

"I don't know," said Summers.

"Well, if we don't find it pretty damn soon," said Red Jack, "we'll all freeze to death out here. I ain't never been this cold in my whole life."

"Let's stop somewhere and build us a fire," said Skeeter.

"Where?" said Thane Savage. "Look around. There ain't no shelter nowhere in sight. We just got to keep on moving, that's all."

"This is a hell of a fix you got us in, Savage," said Summers. "This was all your damned idea."

Savage pulled back on his reins and stopped his horse. Then he swung a leg over to dismount.

"Hey," said Summers. "What the hell are you doing?"

"You don't want to freeze," said Savage, "you'll do the same."

Savage untied the blanket roll from behind his saddle. He pulled the roll off and dropped it on the ground, where he unrolled it, taking out all the things that were packed in there and stuffing them into his saddlebags. Then he wrapped the blanket around his shoulders and mounted up again.

"It's better than nothing," he said. Then he started riding forward again.

"Wait up," said Puckett. He dismounted to follow the example of Savage, and then the others did, too.

"You catch up," Savage called out over his shoulder. He kept riding. He hadn't gone far, though, when he stopped again. In another minute or two the others, wrapped in their blankets, rode up beside him. Still he just sat there.

"Well, let's go," said Summers. "We're all ready now."

"Check your six-guns," said Savage.

"What?"

"Check them. Get ready. Someone's coming."

Summers and the others looked ahead,

and then they saw on the far horizon a wagon coming in their direction on the road from Fort Kearney. It was still too far away to tell how many men might be in it.

"We going to take it, Thane?" asked Puckett.

"Hell, yes."

"We don't even know what it's hauling," said Summers. "It might not be worth the trouble."

The wagon was a little closer, and the outlaws could make out at least three men riding in it.

"I bet they at least got coats on," said Savage. "Maybe a few dollars in their pockets."

"I sure do need a coat," said Skeeter.

"Then take out them six-guns now," said Savage, "and hold them ready underneath your blankets. And then just follow my lead."

Dhu spent a little time in the morning buying some more supplies. The cold weather had hit overnight, and he needed a good warm coat and gloves. He also bought a couple of extra pairs of long underwear and two more blankets. He got some more trail food and extra ammunition for his revolver and his rifle, and then he started out on the road for Fort Kearney. He had no proof that Savage and the others had gone that way; but no other way made sense to him.

It was late in the evening of Dhu's first night out of Kansas City. He had crossed into Nebraska Territory, and he was traveling a well-used road. He had been watching the gray sky all day, but suddenly it became black, and then the snow came. It came from the west, and it drove right into his face. He kept going as long as he could, but at last the snow was driving so hard that he no longer knew if it was day or night, and he could not tell whether or not he was keeping to the road. He had to stop. But where?

He felt like a fool for not having found himself a spot to camp at the first sign of snow. It was too hard fighting the wind and the snow in his face, and so he turned his horse around. He thought that he was moving northwest, off of the road, but he wasn't sure. Then he found himself right up against a snowdrift that must have reached as high as his horse's head.

He dismounted, careful to hang tight to the reins, and he started to scoop out a haven on the sheltered side of the drift. The frightened horse was hard to handle, and the scraping was difficult with one hand, but Dhu managed to create a nook in which he and the horse could huddle. He drew the animal into the nook and tied the reins to his own belt in order to free his hands. Then he unsaddled the horse and unrolled his blanket roll. One blanket went over the horse's head and two more on its back. In the protective nook the wind wasn't howling quite as much as before, and the snow wasn't biting into their faces. Soon the horse calmed down.

Dhu spread a couple of blankets for himself on the ground, and he lay down and covered himself up as best he could. He wondered, as he felt himself drifting into sleep, if he would ever wake up again.

Herd McClellan was up and around at last. He was still weak, so he carried a walking stick in each hand. Sam Ed had carved them out of mesquite wood. He had only walked a few steps at a time, from the bed to the table and back at meal times. It had been a major triumph when Maude had allowed him to venture to the outhouse alone. But at last he was up and about.

They had just finished breakfast, and Herd, using his two sticks, walked out on the porch. He drew the air in through his nostrils and let it out of his mouth. Sam Ed came out of the house behind him.

"Winter's coming on," said Herd. "You got enough firewood laid by?"

"We got plenty, Pa."

"What about the hay? You got plenty put up?"

"Pa, we're getting ready for winter. Most everything's done, and what ain't done yet, we're working on it. Me and Ben, we've kept right on top of everything, and the hands has all been working real hard. They're good men. You don't need to be worrying yourself."

"Yeah? Well, maybe I'll ride out today and look things over. I think I can set a horse well enough now. Why don't you run out to the barn and saddle me up that little roan. Bring her over here."

"Pa, there ain't no need. You've only been up on your feet a few days now. Wait a little longer. Everything's under control."

Then Maude's voice came through the screen door. "Herd, you ain't getting on no horse. Not yet. Just put that thought out of your mind right now. Sam Ed."

"Yes, ma'am?"

"Your pa asks you again to saddle him a horse, you check with me before you do it. You hear me?"

"Yes, ma'am."

"Shit," Herd mumbled.

"And watch your language, you old goat."

"Fetch me a chair out here, boy," said Herd. "I think I'll set here on the porch a spell. And bring me my pipe, too."

Sam Ed brought out a straight-backed, cane-bottomed chair, and Herd sat down on it. Then Sam Ed handed his father a pipe and a tobacco pouch. Herd filled the pipe, and Sam Ed gave him some matches. Herd scratched one on a porch post and lit his pipe.

"Well?" he said.

"Yeah?"

"You going to stand around here all day, or you going to get out and get some work done?"

Sam Ed heaved a sigh, gave a shrug of his shoulders, and rolled his eyes toward the sky.

"I'm on the way," he said. He jumped down off the porch and headed for the barn. Herd sat alone and puffed on his pipe for a few minutes. Then he heard the door behind him open and shut again. He glanced over his shoulder to see Katharine coming out. She walked over and stood beside him.

"It's a nice morning," she said.

"Winter's coming," said Herd.

"Yes. It's a little later here than it is back home. I wonder where Dhu is just now."

"Ain't no telling," said Herd. "I reckon when he's ready for us to know, he'll get word to us one way or another. I told him he didn't have to go after those boys. I told him I wouldn't hold him to the promise he made me. I was half out of my mind when I made him make that promise. I'd never done it otherwise. Hell, if anything happens to that boy, I won't never forgive myself."

"It's not your fault, Herd," said Katharine. She reached back to gather her skirts so that she could sit on the porch there beside the old man. "It's Dhu. He's restless, I think. I think he just needed to get away for a while."

He needed to get away from me, she thought, but she couldn't quite bring herself to say that out loud to Herd McClellan. She didn't even like to think about it, to admit it to herself, but she knew that it was true. If anything should happen to Dhu, she thought, it would be at least as much her fault as Herd's. Maybe more.

The door swung open again, and little Nellie Bell came out onto the porch.

"Kate," said the little girl. "Kate. I need to put my baby to bed. She wants to go to sleep."

Katharine looked at her niece. She was clutching a rag doll to her chest.

"Well, all right, sweetie," she said. "Where does she want to go to bed?"

"At my house. Come on."

Katharine took Nellie Bell by the hand and stood up.

"All right," she said. "Let's go. Herd, don't overdo it now. Don't sit up too long today."

"I'm doing just fine," said Herd. "You go on and put the baby to bed."

Dhu woke up to find himself almost covered with snow, but, he mused, he did wake up. That was something. And his horse was still there. The snow had quit, and the large drift had protected him and his horse through the night from the worst of the storm. He dusted most of the snow off his blankets and stood up. Then he took the blankets off his horse. He rubbed the horse's head and neck and patted its shoulders, talking to it to reassure it. Then he shook out the blankets and rolled them up. He saddled the horse and strapped on the blanket roll. Then he mounted up.

Where it had not drifted the snow was only about a foot deep, and the going was not too rough. It didn't seem as cold as it had the night before, probably because the wind was no longer blowing so hard. But Dhu was uncomfortable. His clothes were wet. So were his blankets. He needed a warm, dry place in which to thaw out, but he didn't expect to see such a place for a while. He wasn't even sure that he'd be able to find the road again, but he rode south. If he hadn't totally lost his sense of direction in the snowstorm, he reckoned, he should be north of the road, and not too far away from it either.

Then he saw it. The road was still visible because the snow had piled a little higher on the grass than on the road. He urged the horse forward and onto the road, turning west again.

"Come on, boy," he said.

Ahead he could see nothing but the dim outline of the road receding in the distance. All around was flat. Everything was white. The sky was clear. That much was good. But he was afraid that the combination of the cold and the wet clothes was liable to do him in. He had some dry clothes in his saddlebags, and he wondered if he should try to change them out there in the open. He wondered if he would be worse off exposing his skin to the cold or keeping it enclosed in the wet clothing. He really didn't know. But he kept riding.

Then he saw a change on the far horizon. It looked like the tree-lined bank of a river or stream. It was still a good ways off, and it appeared to be off to the left or south side of the road. As he got closer and saw that it was definitely trees he began angling toward them. Trees would give him some shelter, at least. It seemed to take forever to reach the grove, but when he was finally there he saw that his guess had been right. A small stream ran parallel to the road at this point, and the stream was lined with trees.

Dhu rode into the trees and unsaddled the horse. Then he gathered some fallen branches and built a fire. He took a moment to huddle over the fire and warm himself. Then he stretched a blanket between two trees for a windbreak, and he changed into dry clothes. He hung out the wet clothes and the wet blankets to dry, and he cooked himself a hot meal and made some coffee.

He still didn't know how far he had to go to find a town or even a farmhouse, but life began to look much better than it had just a short while earlier. The horse was doing all right, too. He had dug at the ground with his hoof to find the grass underneath the snow, and he was grazing. Dhu would let him work for his food for a while. Then he would reward him with some oats from the saddlebags.

It was a fairly comfortable and secure-seeming spot, and it would be tempting to linger, but Dhu knew better than to give in to that temptation. When he and the horse were rested, fed, and warmed up a little they would have to be on their way again. There was no way of knowing when the next storm would come, and he sure as hell didn't want to be stranded out in the big, cold middle of nowhere.

Chapter 16

It was a tiny town, but Dhu was glad to see it. There were buildings, and it would be warm inside. He was hungry for a good hot meal, and after that, he thought, a drink would be good. As he rode into the town he noted that he could just about take it all in at a glance. He spotted a place that bore a sign that said EATS, then rode on past it to the livery stable.

The big barn door was closed. Dhu dismounted there in front of it and pulled it open a few inches.

"Hello," he hollered. "Anyone here?"

"I'm coming."

In another minute a squat man in dirty clothes appeared at the door.

"Yeah?" he said.

"Can you feed my horse and board him for the night?"

"Pay in advance," said the man.

"Sure," said Dhu. He dug into his pockets and pulled out some change.

"Treat him right and I'll pay a little extra when I pick him up."

"I'll give him the best I got," said the dirty little man.

"You notice most of the strangers who ride through this town?"

The man cocked his head and squinted at Dhu.

"Most, I'd say."

"Did you see five men ride through recently? I'd guess not more than a week ago. Southerners. Two of them are cowboys from Texas. The last I knew they were riding a black, a roan, a gray, a buckskin, and a paint."

The man hesitated, and Dhu had the distinct impression that he was trying to decide how to answer the question. What was there to decide? He had either seen them or he hadn't.

"About a week ago, you say?"

"More or less," said Dhu.

"Seems like some riders come through here about then. I can't say if it was them. I didn't pay that much attention to what they was riding."

"All right," said Dhu. "I'll see you later."

He walked across the street and back west for a little ways to the place called EATS, and he went inside. There were a few others in there, but the place was far from busy. Dhu looked around quickly and selected a table. A man in a greasy apron walked over.

"What can I get you?" he said.

"Coffee to start with," said Dhu.

He ate steak and eggs and fried potatoes and biscuits, and he had to admit that the man was a good cook. He was paying the man for the meal when he happened to glance out the window just in time to see the dirty man from the stable running along. He was going in the direction of the stable, so he must have gone somewhere else and was hurrying back. Dhu went outside and stood for a moment looking up and down the street.

There were two saloons. He picked the nearest one. It was just across the street. He walked across and went inside. Three tables were occupied, one of them with a card game, and four men were standing at the bar. Dhu went to the bar, and a burly bartender approached him.

"Whiskey," said Dhu.

The bartender gave him a curious look, hesitated a moment, then went for the whiskey bottle and a glass. To do so he had to walk past the other four men at the bar. They were clustered together at the far end of the bar from where Dhu waited.

"Hey," said one of the four, and he gestured for the bartender to lean over close. Dhu saw the man speak low to the bartender, and he saw them both shoot glances in his direction. The rest of their conversation was still low, but Dhu could make it out.

"Well, I thought maybe he might be," said the bartender, "but then I couldn't be sure."

"Yeah, well, maybe you ought to make sure," said the other.

The bartender nodded, glanced at Dhu again, picked up the bottle and the glass, and walked back along the length of the bar. He stopped in front of Dhu and stood looking at him from across the bar. He still held the bottle and the glass but made no move to pour the whiskey. He looked nervous.

"Is something wrong here?" said Dhu.

"Yeah. Well, maybe. I don't know yet for sure."

"Spit it out," said Dhu.

"All right. Are you a Indian?"

"Mister," said Dhu, "whatever I am, I'm not ashamed of it, but I don't think it's any of your business. I can only think of one question you have a right to ask me, and that's whether or not I have the price of a drink."

Dhu reached into his pocket and pulled out a handful of change, which he dumped on the bar in front of him.

"I have the price. Pour the drink."

The bartender poured a drink and walked back down to the other men.

"He ain't no Indian," he said.

"How do you know?"

"Hell, Rafe, he don't talk like no Indian, and he's got plenty of cash."

Rafe tossed down what was left of his own drink, then turned to stare at Dhu.

"By God," he said, "he looks like a damned Indian to me."

"Don't start no trouble, Rafe," said the bartender.

"Shut up," said Rafe, and he started walking toward Dhu. He walked about half the distance and stopped. "Hey, you. Indian."

Dhu took a sip of his drink and gave Rafe a casual glance.

"Are you talking to me?"

"You see any other Indians in here?"

Dhu took another sip of his drink.

"Yeah, I'm talking to you. What reservation you come off of anyway?"

"None, mister, and I didn't come in here

to swap small talk with you either."

Dhu finished his drink. Rafe pointed up toward the wall behind the bar.

"Can you read?" he said.

"Probably better than you can," said Dhu.

"Read that."

Dhu glanced in the direction Rafe was pointing. There was a sign on the wall: NO INDIANS ALLOWED.

"Well?" said Rafe.

"Well what?"

"You read it?"

"I read it."

"Well, what are you?"

"I'm an American," said Dhu.

"Well, what kind?"

"Is there more than one kind?"

"Damn it, are you a goddamn Indian or ain't you?"

"I don't exactly know what an Indian is," said Dhu. "I'm half white and half Cherokee. Now what are you? I'd guess at least half human, but I'm not sure about the other half."

"Damn you," said Rafe.

"Cherokee," said one of the other men. "That's one of them civilized tribes."

"That's why he talks like that," said another.

"Civilized or not," said Rafe, "the damn

186

sign says no Indians. Now you can either get out of here right now or be carried out a little later."

"Bartender," said Dhu, "I think I'll have another drink."

"The hell you will," said Rafe.

Just then the front door swung open and a man in a long winter coat stepped inside.

"What's going on here?" he said in a booming voice.

"You stay out of this, Barjac," said Rafe. "We're just fixing to kick a smartass Indian out of here, that's all."

Barjac walked steadily across the room toward a point just between Dhu and Rafe.

"Go back to your drink, Rafe," he said.

"Damn it," said Rafe.

Barjac didn't seem to hurry, but two more long strides took him to within striking distance. His right hand whipped the hat off his head and slapped it across Rafe's face. His left executed a quick cross-draw, and the muzzle of his revolver was pressed into the belly of Rafe.

"I said go back to your drink, Rafe," said Barjac, and this time his voice was low and calm. Rafe moved back to huddle with his friends, and Barjac turned toward Dhu, putting away his revolver.

"I came looking for you," he said.

"And found me just in time, I'd say," said Dhu. "One of us was about to kill the other."

"It seemed that way. My name's Barjac. I'm the sheriff here. If you don't mind strolling over to my office with me, I'd like to have a talk with you."

"I don't mind, Sheriff," said Dhu, "but I had just ordered another drink right before you walked in. I didn't get it."

"Bring him his drink," said Barjac.

The bartender brought the bottle and poured Dhu's glass full. Dhu shoved some change at him.

"Thanks," he said. He tipped back his head and sipped at the drink. "Be with you in a minute, Sheriff."

"I'm in no hurry."

In the sheriff's office Barjac poured himself a cup of coffee and offered one to Dhu, but Dhu declined. Barjac pointed to a chair, and Dhu sat down. Then the sheriff sat on the edge of his desk. He slurped at the hot coffee, then set the cup down on the desk.

"I told you my name," he said. "You mind giving yours?"

"Dhu Walker."

"Where you from, Mr. Walker?"

"Texas."

"You mind telling me what you're doing in these parts?"

"Sheriff," said Dhu, "I rode into this town minding my own business, and I've even spread a little money around since I've been here. I've been harassed, and now I'm being questioned by the sheriff. Do you mind telling me what this is all about?"

"Well, sir," said Barjac, "you said you come from Texas. I heard Rafe call you an Indian, and you do kind of have the look of an Indian about you."

"I'm Cherokee," said Dhu, "and half white. I'm also part owner of a ranch in Texas."

"I've been down in your part of the country, Walker. Indian Territory. That where you're from?"

"That's right."

"Have you ever been up this way before?"

"No."

"Well, folks up here have a real different attitude toward you people than they do down where you come from. You saw the sign on the wall?"

"I saw it."

"Well, if you'd been over to the other saloon in town, you'd have found one that

189

says, 'No dogs or Indians allowed.' "

"That sort of explains the harassment in the saloon," said Dhu. "It doesn't explain your interest."

"I heard that you came into town asking about five men."

"Oh, that's right. I saw the stable man running down the street."

"Yeah. He came and told me."

"Okay. It's true."

"Who are they, and what's your connection with them?"

Dhu took out the makings and rolled himself a smoke. He struck a match on the arm of the chair in which he sat, and he lit the cigarette. Then he looked up at Barjac through a cloud of blue-gray smoke.

"One of the five men is a Texan named Thane Savage," he said. "A while back he shot one of my partners from ambush. Then he went to town, he and another out-of-work cowboy, and they killed and robbed a saloonkeeper. They're wanted in Texas for robbery, attempted murder, and murder. I followed them out of Texas, through the Choctaw Nation, Arkansas, the Cherokee Nation, and eventually all the way up here. By the way, they're also wanted in the Choctaw Nation and in Arkansas. Robbery and murder. And if a certain sheriff I met in Arkansas did what he said he was going to do, they ought to be wanted by the federal government by now as well."

"You know the other names?"

"One's Arlie Puckett. He's another Texan. He's been with Savage almost from the beginning. They picked up the others in Fort Gibson. They were whiskey runners from Arkansas. One's named Charlie Summers. The other two are called Skeeter and Red Jack. Now you know just about all that I know. Are you going to tell me why you're interested?"

"They rode through here about a week ago, Walker," said Barjac. "They were noticed, but that's about all. They didn't stop. Just rode through. That should have made me suspect something. Everybody stops. Especially in this kind of weather. I should have noticed the coats, too. You see, four men drove a wagon out of here earlier that same day. The next day their bodies were found out on the road. They'd been shot to death, and their coats were gone. These five you're chasing murdered our friends for their coats."

"Did you go after them?" asked Dhu.

"Sure. But it was too late. They got right out of my jurisdiction."

"Border lines don't stop me, Sheriff," said Dhu. "Can you tell me where they were headed?"

"I think I can pin it down pretty damn close for you," said Barjac. "Just a minute. Let me pull out this old map here."

"Barjac," said Dhu. "I think I will have a cup of that coffee of yours, if you don't mind."

Chapter

17

Barjac poured Dhu some coffee, then pulled a map out of a drawer and rolled it out on top of the clutter that was already there on the desktop. Dhu held down one edge of the curly paper.

"Now here we are," said Barjac. "Right here. Off over here's Fort Kearney. But that gang you're after didn't head for Kearney. They headed due north. Right here. I followed them up this far, and I couldn't go any farther. They crossed into Dakota Territory. That's out of my jurisdiction. That's where I turned back."

Dhu saw something in Barjac's face that told him the man had hated quitting, that he had really wanted to go on after Savage and the others. He took a sip of the coffee the sheriff had given him. It was strong and bitter.

"Well," he said, "I guess that's my trail, then. I'll hit it first thing in the morning. Thanks for the information."

"It's a long ride up there to the border," said Barjac. "And from there we don't know where they went. Got no idea."

"Well, if I keep close enough," said Dhu, "I figure they'll show themselves again sooner or later."

"Yeah," said Barjac. "They will."

Dhu stayed the night in a fleabag hotel and got up early the next morning. He bought himself a good breakfast, then picked up his horse at the livery stable and left town going north, following the trail the sheriff had pointed out for him. Dakota Territory, he thought, and he wondered if he would see any Sioux Indians along the way.

Barjac stood watching through his office window as Dhu rode out of town. Then he poured himself another cup of coffee and sat down behind his desk. He was sipping coffee and shuffling papers when he heard the sound of pounding hooves outside. Probably just some frisky cowboys, he thought, but he wanted to be sure. He got up and walked back to the window.

Rafe and his three companions from the saloon were in a big hurry to get somewhere. Barjac stepped out of the office and stood on the boardwalk to watch them. They headed north. It could be a coincidence, the sheriff thought, but he remembered the incident at the saloon and the hatred in Rafe's voice and in his face. They were following Dhu Walker. Barjac couldn't think of any other reason the cowboys would be headed out of town in that direction.

He went back inside, strapped on his revolver, and got his rifle out of the rack. He put on his coat and stuffed the pockets with boxes of bullets. Then he grabbed his hat and headed for the door.

In a matter of minutes he was mounted up and ready to ride out after Rafe, but instead he rode back to his office. He didn't go back inside, though. He sat there in his saddle and pulled out his watch to check the time. He looked down the street, watching and waiting impatiently as he tucked the watch back away. In a few more minutes a man came strolling down the walk. When he got close enough Barjac yelled at him.

"George, hurry it up, will you?"

George seemed to snap to attention for a moment. Then he trotted on down the walk to stop in front of the sheriff. A deputy's badge was pinned on the outside of George's coat.

"What is it, Sheriff?" he asked.

"You're in charge here," said Barjac. "I'm going out of town."

"Where you going?"

"If I'd wanted you to know, I'd have told you, now wouldn't I? All you need to know is that I'm out of town, and you're in charge."

"For how long?"

"Until I get back and tell you different."

Without another word Barjac turned his horse and rode away, leaving George standing alone in front of the office scratching his head. Soon Barjac was out on the prairie headed north. The country was flat grassland, and he could see ahead for a good long way. He should be able to spot them in a short while, he thought. But he didn't, and he began to worry. By noon he began to get hungry, but he decided that his stomach would just have to wait. He kept riding.

It was about midday when Dhu found himself on the south bank of a river. It was a peculiar-looking river to the man from the wooded hill country of the Cherokee Nation. Even the Red River, which divided the Indian territory from Texas, was tree-lined. This river had no trees. It just wandered through the flat grassland. It did run

196

through a sort of a river valley, but not much of one.

Even so, Dhu thought that it would be as good a place to stop as any in this cold, desolate north country. He was hungry, and his horse needed a rest. He rode down to the riverbank and dismounted. The horse started to drink the yellow river water. Dhu knelt down, tasted it, and decided that it was all right. He was just as glad, though, that he had plenty of water for himself in his canteen, and if he needed more, he decided, he would melt some snow.

When the horse had drunk its fill Dhu pulled the saddle off and, leaving the reins to trail on the ground, let it graze. One thing, he thought: There was plenty of grass, even under the snow. He looked around, but he didn't see anything with which to build a fire, so he ate a little cold camp food, some jerky and hardtack, and he washed it down with cold water. He thought about stretching out on the ground to rest, but the ground was still snow-covered. He would have to unroll his blankets to make it halfway comfortable, and he didn't intend to stay long enough to make that worthwhile. Besides, he didn't want to roll up wet blankets when the time came to leave again.

It was too cold to make the short stop really restful for Dhu, so as soon as he thought that he'd given the horse enough of a break he decided to saddle up and move out again. He hoped that by sundown he would find a more suitable place for a real camp.

He bent to pick up the saddle just as a rifle shot sounded, and he made a dive and rolled in the snow. Looking up the slight rise from the river valley, he saw four men with rifles. They were on the ground, their horses standing back behind them. Dhu glanced back toward his saddle. His rifle was still over there, and he had rolled some distance away from it. Another rifle shot sounded, and Dhu saw the snow kicked up by the bullet just a few feet to his left. He drew out his revolver. It would be a long shot, but it was all he had.

Up on top of the rise a man raised his rifle to his shoulder. Dhu fired at him. He missed, but the shot came close enough to make the man flinch and shoot wild. Dhu's horse was nickering and fidgeting nervously. He hoped that it would stay put, and he hoped that no stray bullet would find it.

Dhu fired again, his own shot going wild.

Then he rolled quickly to his left as three more rifle shots sounded. He scooted himself down into the snow in a slight depression there in the ground in an attempt to make himself as difficult a target as he could. It wasn't much cover from the men with rifles who were on higher ground.

He was in a desperate situation, and he knew it. He couldn't hit his attackers from that distance with his revolver. He had already wasted two shots. And sooner or later one of the four rifles up there would find its mark. He couldn't think of anything except a wild dash for his own rifle, and that would be real risky.

Then he heard another rifle shot, but it sounded from farther off, from back behind his attackers, and no sooner had that information soaked into his head than he saw one of the men up there drop his rifle and fall forward. He didn't know what was happening, but he thought fast and took advantage of the situation. He scrambled to his feet and, in a crouch, ran for his rifle. Jerking it out of its scabbard, he ran a few more steps. More shots sounded, and Dhu felt something thud into his left thigh. He knew that he'd been hit. Throwing himself to the ground, he rolled to his right. Then from a prone position in the snow he aimed and fired, and another of his attackers dropped. That left only two, and they were suddenly confused, trapped.

One faced Dhu, and the other faced away. Dhu took another bead, but before he could fire he heard another distant shot ring out, and the man he was aiming at fell back and rolled a few feet down toward the river. The remaining man ran for his horse. He had just gotten into his saddle when another shot knocked him back out of it. Dhu stood up, hopping on his right foot, rifle in hand, and stared at the ridge. The silence was ominous.

His horse nickered and stamped, and he spoke low to reassure it.

"It's okay," he said. "Calm down. It seems to be all over now. We'll just wait a minute here and see who shows up. Take it easy, old boy. Take it easy."

Then a rider appeared above. Horse and man presented Dhu with only a silhouette. Dhu squinted in the glaring light of the sun on snow. Then the rider waved an arm.

"You, Walker. You all right down there?" he yelled.

"Yeah," said Dhu. "Thanks to you."

The rider started down toward Dhu, and in a moment Dhu recognized Barjac. He put down his rifle as Barjac dismounted.

"Who were they?" said Dhu.

"Old Rafe and that bunch from the saloon last night. They're all dead."

"Nice folks you have up here in the north country," Dhu said, and he hopped over to his saddle and sat down on it. He found the hole in his trousers where the bullet had torn through and ripped it open wider to examine the wound.

"You've been hit," said Barjac. "I thought you said you were all right."

"It's not bad," said Dhu. "Anyhow, it missed the bone."

"Yeah. Well, you'd better let me take a look at it." Barjac walked over to Dhu and knelt in the snow. "It's just a flesh wound," he said, "but it's bleeding pretty good. We'll have to try to put a stop to that."

Dhu pulled open his saddlebags. "I've got some clean bandannas in here," he said, and he shoved his hand inside to search for them.

Barjac tore Dhu's trouser leg the rest of the way around and looked at the leg more closely.

"It looks like the bullet went all the way through," he said. "At least we won't have to dig the damn thing out. Hold on a minute." He stood up and walked to his horse. Then he reached into his own saddlebags and produced a bottle of whiskey.

"That's real handy," said Dhu.

"I never travel without it."

Barjac moved back to Dhu's side and poured a generous portion of whiskey into the bullet hole. Dhu flinched and gasped out loud. Barjac handed the bottle to Dhu, and Dhu took a long drink. He handed the bottle back, and Barjac took a quick swallow. "That's good whiskey," he said. "Now hand me that bandanna."

He bound up the wound and stood up.

"You got any spare trousers in that pack?"

"Yeah."

"Better get them on before you freeze your damn leg."

Dhu dug out the trousers and changed. While he was struggling with that chore Barjac rode back up the rise. He pulled the saddles and the harness off the horses up there and turned them loose. Then he rode back down to where Dhu was waiting.

"What about those bodies up there?" asked Dhu.

"They won't go anywhere, and in this weather they'll keep."

Dhu shrugged. "Barjac," he said, "how'd you happen along here just in time anyhow?"

"Didn't just happen," said Barjac. "I saw that bunch ride out of town after you this morning, and it made me a little suspicious. Thought I'd better trail along and see what they were up to."

"Well, I'm sure glad you did. They had me in a spot. Likely they'd have killed me if you hadn't popped up back there when you did."

"You got anything to eat?" said Barjac. "I was so worried about your well-being that I didn't take the time to pack any food this morning, and killing always makes me hungry."

"Some jerky and hard bread," said Dhu. "This is a cold camp."

"Yeah. In more ways than one."

Barjac ate, and then Dhu struggled to his feet and started to pick up his saddle.

"Here," said Barjac. "Let me do that."

"Thanks," said Dhu. The thigh was beginning to throb with a dull pain. Barjac got the horse saddled, and Dhu hobbled over to it and took the reins.

"Well," he said, "I guess I'll head on. Thanks again, Barjac."

"You going ahead like that?"

"Why not?"

"Don't you think you ought to ride back with me and get a doctor to look at that bullet wound?"

"Anything he could do that you didn't do already?"

"You ought to at least take it easy for a while and let it heal."

"Time heals," said Dhu, "and time will pass on the trail just the same as in town."

"You're a stubborn son of a bitch," said Barjac. He stood and watched while Dhu pulled himself up into the saddle with a groan. Wincing with the pain, Dhu settled into the seat.

"You think you can ride with that?" said Barjac.

"Yeah," said Dhu. "I think so."

"Well, then, I think I'll just ride along with you," said the sheriff. "This trail gets a little hard to follow on up north of here."

Dhu looked at the sheriff for a moment.

"Suit yourself," he said.

Barjac rode into the river headed for the north bank, and Dhu glanced back toward the rise where the four dead men were lying.

"What about them?" he asked.

"Leave them," said Barjac.

Dhu shrugged and followed Barjac into the water. He's the sheriff, he thought, and this is his country. Leave them there.

Chapter

18

Skeeter rode wrapped in a blanket, and he was shivering.

"Hey," he said, his voice whiny, "let me wear one of them coats for a while. It ain't fair for me to be the one to have to go without a coat all the time. I helped kill those bastards back there. I helped to get them coats. You ought to let me wear one some of the time."

No one bothered to respond to his plea. They rode on in silence.

"I ought to get to wear one for part of the time, at least," he said. "Goddamnit, I'm cold, I'm about to freeze. I might freeze to death."

"Aw, shut up," said Summers. "We'll find another coat somewhere along the way. Then you can have one, too. Just pull that blanket up real close, and you'll be all right."

"It ain't fair. Shit," said Skeeter.

"Damn it," said Savage. "You think these

coats is keeping us warm? You think they're all that warm? There ain't no way to keep warm in this here damn cold. We're all of us cold."

He yanked hard on the reins, pulling his horse to a sudden halt, and he started taking off his coat.

"Here. Just to keep you quiet. You take this goddamn coat and give me that blanket, and I don't want to hear no more out of you. Not another goddamn word. You understand?"

He tossed the coat at Skeeter, who fumbled for a moment with coat and blanket, then tossed the blanket over to Savage. Savage wrapped the blanket around his shoulders.

"Thanks," said Skeeter.

"Shut up," said Savage. "Come on. We got to find a sign of civilization somewhere before much longer."

"We should have stopped at that town back yonder," said Skeeter, buttoning up the coat.

"Right after we killed four men just down the road?" said Savage. "That would've been real smart, now, wouldn't it? Besides, I give you my damn coat so you'd shut up your damn whining. Now shut it up."

Skeeter eased his mount up close to Summers and rode along for a while in sulking silence. He watched Savage until Savage was well ahead. Then he spoke in a low voice to Summers.

"When did we decide that he was our boss anyhow?" he said. "Did we decide that?"

"Take it easy," said Summers. "His time will come."

"Well, it can't come any too soon for me," muttered Skeeter. "You just give me the word, and I'm ready anytime. Any damn time."

"Say," said Summers, suddenly speaking out loudly for all to hear, "anyone got any idea where the hell we're at by now?"

When no one else answered, Savage spoke again. "No, I ain't," he said, "but we're going to find us someplace up here to hole up for the winter. I got a idea that the winter's going to be long and hard in this part of the country. If we don't find us someplace here before long, we'll all likely freeze to death up here. And that ain't just whining neither."

It was about a half hour later when Red Jack spotted the curling wisp of gray smoke in the air ahead.

"Hey. Look up there," he said, pointing.

"Looks like it's coming out of a chimbley to me," said Arlie Puckett.

"Come on," said Savage, kicking his horse to hurry it up. "Let's get our ass to that fire."

The land was still flat, but there were clumps of trees here and there, and the road was beginning to wind around a bit. Off in the distance the outlaws could see the mountains beginning to rise up out of the flat country. They raced around a bend in the road, and then they could see the small log structure up ahead, smoke rising from its chimney.

"I told you," shouted Puckett.

As they got closer they could see a small barn and corral behind the building, several horses tied up to a hitching rail in front.

"That ain't just a house, is it?" said Puckett.

Then they were close enough to read the crudely lettered sign that was tacked up above the front door, those who could read.

"Trading post," said Summers.

"Well, let's check the son of a bitch out," said Savage. "See what they've got to trade for."

They dismounted and hastily tied their

horses to the already crowded rail. Skeeter ran, and so he was the first one to the door, and he practically burst inside. Several heads turned to see who had come in, and Skeeter stopped just inside the doorway, a bit startled by his own abruptness and by the reaction from the strangers inside. Then Savage was pushing him from behind.

"Don't block the damn door," he said. Skeeter stepped aside, and Savage strode on in, followed closely by the others. Along the back wall of the room there was a counter or bar. Three round tables with chairs and several free-standing shelves cluttered with a variety of goods filled the rest of the crowded room. Two men sat at one table, and one at another, and a man stood behind the counter. On the wall to the right was a large rock fireplace, an overbuilt fire roaring on its hearth. Skeeter headed for it and backed up to the fire, lifting up the tail of his coat.

"I may never be warm again," he said.

A long moment of silence followed, interrupted at last by the man behind the counter.

"Howdy, gents," he said. "Welcome."

"Howdy," said Savage. "You sell whiskey in here?"

"I ain't a saloon," said the man. "I don't sell drinks, but I can sell it to you by the bottle. If you got the price."

"That's just fine," said Savage. "Can you loan us five glasses to drink it out of, or do we have to pass the bottle around?"

"Sure. I got glasses."

The man reached under the counter and produced a bottle and five glasses, and Savage put some money on the counter.

"Hey, boys," he said. "Get these glasses here and take them over to that table there."

He took the bottle, and he walked to the one unoccupied table and sat down. Summers and Red Jack brought the glasses, and Savage poured each one full of whiskey.

"You want some of this, Skeeter," he said, "get your ass over here. I sure ain't serving it to you."

Skeeter reluctantly left his spot before the fire and went to the table for his whiskey.

Savage took his glass with him and walked back over to the counter.

"Say," he said, "what the hell are you doing with this place way out here, anyway? I mean, is there a town somewhere close by?"

"Ain't no town," said the man, "unless you want to count Sioux camps."

"Well, where do you get all your business from? They ain't that many travelers along this little old road, is they?"

"Injun trade," said the man. "We're on the Sioux reservation here."

"Oh. Injun trade, huh? Where I come from there ain't no Injuns. We run them all off or killed them."

"Where you from?"

"Texas," said Savage. "You got any good coats for sale here?"

"Right over there," said the man, pointing to a counter against the wall opposite the fireplace. "Just pick out what you like."

"Yeah. I will in just a minute. I don't suppose you fix meals to sell."

"I got a pot of stew on in the back room. Ten cents a bowl."

"Dish us up five bowls," said Savage.

"For a extra nickel I'll toss in a chunk of sourdough bread."

"Yeah. Five of them."

While the man went to dish up the stew Savage walked over to pick out a coat. He found one and tried it on. It suited him, so he pulled it off and carried it to the counter. Just as he laid it down the man came back out with five bowls of stew and five pieces of bread on a tray. He carried them over to the table where Savage's companions waited.

"That's seventy-five cents," he said. "You want the coat, too?"

"Yeah," said Savage. "I'll pay up when we're done here. We'll be needing to pick up some supplies for the trail, too. Just keep adding it all up."

They finished their bowls of stew in short order, and Savage poured another round of drinks.

"Hey," he shouted, "how about refills on that stew?"

The man brought his tray and picked up the bowls. As he was returning to the back room Savage turned to the man who was sitting alone.

"Howdy," he said.

"Hello," said the man.

"Where would five men lay up for the winter up in them mountains?"

"I don't know," said the man. "I wouldn't go up there this time of year myself."

"Where do you stay?"

"I live over at the agency. I work for the Indian agent there."

"Oh, yeah?"

"Hey, Tex."

Savage turned to face the voice. It came from one of the two men seated at the other table.

"You headed up in them mountains, you say?"

"That's right."

"Planning on doing some hunting, are you?"

Savage hesitated a moment.

"How'd you guess?" he said.

"That's about the only reason I can think of why anybody'd want to go up there this time of year. That or digging for gold, and there ain't no gold up there. I've looked. Or else he might be wanting to hide out from someone."

"We're hunters," said Savage.

"Well, there is a cabin up there about a day's ride from here. Just follow the trail. You can't miss it."

"Nobody lives there?" said Savage.

"An old trapper named Bates built it and stayed there for some time. Squirrely Bates, they called him. He's gone now. The place is abandoned, but the last time I was up that way it was still livable. Nobody wouldn't object if you was to just move in the place."

"Thanks, friend," said Savage. "Maybe we'll check it out."

The man with the stew came back then, and Savage and the gang busied themselves once again with eating. When Savage had finished his second bowl of stew he leaned over close to Charlie Summers.

"Charlie," he said, "be ready for anything when I make my move. And tell the other boys, too, if you can keep it quiet."

He gathered up the five bowls and walked toward the counter. The man was sitting back there, and he started to get up to take the bowls.

"Just take it easy there, partner," said Savage. "We had you jumping up and down enough. I'll put these here dirty dishes away for you."

"I'll get them."

"No," Savage insisted. "It ain't no trouble."

He stepped into the back room and put the bowls down. Then he pulled out his revolver and cocked it. He stepped out of the room again, aimed, and fired, hitting the man behind the counter in the side of the head. The man fell over sideways without a sound. Then guns came out all over the room, but the Savage gang was too much for the other three. They had been ready. The others were taken by surprise.

Charlie Summers shot the lone man in

the chest, knocking him over backwards in his chair. Savage and Skeeter both shot one of the other men as he clawed for a weapon underneath his coat, and Red Jack and Puckett both shot the last one.

When the firing stopped Skeeter put his hands to his ears.

"God damn," he said. "That was loud. It's still ringing in my ears."

Arlie Puckett walked over to stand across the counter from Savage.

"Thane," he said, "what did we do that for?"

"Did you want to give all your hard-earned cash to this old cheating bastard?" said Savage.

"Well, no. I guess not."

Savage picked up the coat he had left on the counter and pulled it on.

"I got me a new coat," he said. "Why don't the rest of you get new ones for your-selves? That way nobody won't ever catch us in them ones with bullet holes and blood on them."

They all grabbed new coats.

"I think I seen a wagon out back when we rode up," said Savage. "A couple of you boys fetch it out front and hook up a team to it. We'll load it up with all the supplies we need for the winter. By the time it thaws out again in this damn country won't nobody remember who we are."

"Where we going, Thane?" said Puckett.

"We're going to move into old Squirrely Bates's place," said Savage. "It's just setting there waiting for us. Didn't you hear the man?"

Chapter

19

Barjac stopped his horse, and Dhu wondered what was on the sheriff's mind. As far as he could tell, they were in the middle of nowhere on a trail that might as well lead to the edge of the world. He pulled up beside Barjac, waiting for an explanation. Barjac was just staring ahead.

"You see that rock up there?" said Barjac.

"Sure."

"On the other side of that is Dakota Territory, more specifically the Sioux reservation."

Dhu looked ahead. He could continue riding north. He could turn east or west. He could stay on a trail or follow a road or go across country. Which way had the Savage gang gone? He had no idea. He was in a strange country far from home.

"Well," he said, "I have to go on. Can you suggest a direction for me to take?"

"I think so," said Barjac. "I'd guess that

they followed the trail. Up ahead a few miles it runs into a T. My guess is that they took the turn west. East leads to the agency for the Sioux Indians. Not much else. The west road goes by a trading post and then winds on up into the mountains."

"I'll try the west road," said Dhu. "Thanks, Barjac."

Barjac opened his coat and removed the badge from his vest. He turned and opened the saddlebag on his right side and dropped the star into it, then refastened the strap. Dhu watched with curiosity. Barjac buttoned his coat back and straightened up, then urged his horse forward.

"Let's go, then," he said.

"Wait a minute," said Dhu. "What are you doing? You told me before that you followed them this far and quit. They're out of your jurisdiction."

"You saw me take that badge off, didn't you?" said Barjac.

"If you didn't want to follow them the first time, what makes you so determined now?"

Barjac sighed and shot Dhu an exasperated look.

"I ain't all that sure myself," he said. "Maybe seeing you come all this way because of what happened to a friend of yours. Those four men in the wagon, they were friends of mine. Maybe just knowing what you're up to made me feel the limitations my job put on me, and maybe I'm sick and tired of it. I don't know. What the hell do you care anyway? Are you so much of a loner you want to take on five men all by yourself?"

Dhu climbed down off his horse with a groan. The leg was still stiff and sore. He rolled himself a cigarette, scratched a match on his saddlehorn, and lit up. Then he looked up at Barjac through a wavering cloud of smoke.

"You're used to barking out orders to folks, aren't you?"

"Not without the badge, Walker. Don't worry about that. I won't try to take over and run things."

Dhu took another drag on his cigarette and then expelled the smoke. He stood up and looked around at the cold, desolate country, and he wondered what he would find ahead.

"Well, Walker," said Barjac, "what do you say? Are you going to let me ride along with you?"

"Sure," said Dhu. He tossed away the cigarette and limped back around to the left side of his horse. "You can even lead the way. Let's go."

Riding the long trail north alongside this Barjac, Dhu wondered again about his own motivations. The sheriff had as much as said that Dhu's loyalty to a friend had shamed him into taking off his badge and taking up the pursuit he had previously abandoned. But Dhu wasn't at all sure that his own motive for this extended manhunt had been so noble.

Why, he asked himself, was he so dogged, so determined, so near fanatical about it? Even Herd McClellan had urged him to forget about it, had just about apologized for sending Dhu after Savage in the first place. And Herd was all right. Barjac's friends were dead. On that basis, Barjac's reasons for this trip made more sense than did Dhu's.

He thought back over the last several months, and he reminded himself that he had been restless. He had wondered about the source of that restlessness and had never come up with an answer. He had worried that perhaps the war had instilled deep inside him a lust for action, for violence. He hoped that was not the case.

Then there was Katharine. He had not thought that he left the LWM in search of

Savage in an effort to get away from her. He had not thought that. But he realized that he had been more comfortable once he got away. But now that he had been away for so long — it seemed like an eternity — he found that he was missing her. He found himself thinking about her at night just before dropping off to sleep.

He missed the McClellans, too, all of them, and he even, he admitted just a little reluctantly, missed Ben Lacey, the ignorant Iowa farm boy. And then he startled himself with the realization that he had just told himself that he would have to learn to think better of Ben, because Ben might easily become his brother-in-law.

He tried to put those thoughts out of his mind. He knew that whatever the reasons, he meant to finish this manhunt, and he was much more likely to have a future to contemplate if he could keep his mind on the business at hand.

It was noon the next day when they reached the end of the road, the place where the road turned either east or west. They turned west and rode for another hour. Then they saw riders coming. Dhu pushed back his coat for easy access to his revolver, and Barjac did the same. They moved to opposite sides of the road from each other and waited. The riders came closer.

"Soldiers," said Barjac.

Both men relaxed. They moved ahead slowly to meet the approaching troopers. A sergeant, obviously in charge, held up a hand and halted the squad, and Dhu and Barjac moved on up close and stopped.

"Hello, Sergeant," said Barjac.

"Good afternoon, gentlemen," said the sergeant. "May I ask your business here? You do know that you're on a government reservation?"

"Well," said Barjac, "we think we're just passing through. We're looking for five men. Fugitives from justice."

"Are you lawmen?"

Dhu looked at Barjac, wondering how the lawman would respond to the question.

"No," said Barjac. "We're private citizens. These men killed four of my friends down in Nebraska Territory. They shot this man's partner in Texas."

The sergeant looked at Dhu for a moment. "You've followed these men all the way from Texas?" he asked.

Dhu had only followed Savage and Puckett all the way from Texas, but he didn't think it would do any good to explain all the details.

"Well, yeah," he said. "North Texas."

"I probably shouldn't say this," said the sergeant, "but if you can get them before the United States Army decides to send out a patrol after them, well, good luck to you."

"Will the army send out a patrol?" asked Barjac.

"There's a trading post several miles west of here," said the sergeant. "That's where we've just come from. Two days ago some Indians came into the agency. They'd gone to the trading post for supplies. They found three dead men there. Shot to death. A fourth one was dying from a shot in the chest. He said five men did it. White men. Southerners. He said they were headed for Squirrely Bates's cabin in the mountains. That's off the reservation. So I guess if you're following these same five men, you are just passing through."

"It sounds like the work of the men we're following," said Dhu. "Where is this cabin?"

"Bates's? Just keep on this road. You'll pass right by the trading post. We left a man there temporarily in charge. Just keep going. You'll come to Squirrely's cabin."

"How far?" asked Barjac.

"From the trading post I'd say thirty, forty miles. A good hard day's ride."

"Why aren't you going after them right now?" asked Barjac.

"The Indians told us what they found, and I was ordered to go check it out. If I found it to be true, I was to bury the dead and leave a man to keep the post open, then report back. I'm on the way back. After I've made my report I expect new orders to go after the perpetrators."

"Thanks, Sergeant," said Barjac.

The squad rode on. Dhu and Barjac turned in their saddles and watched them for a moment.

"It sounds like this could be the end of the trail," said Dhu.

"How's that?"

"Sounds like they're finally planning to hole up. I'll get them this time."

"*We'll* get them," said Barjac. "Let's go."

Thane Savage was out of the cabin. He'd gone to the woods out back to answer a call of nature. The others were lounging about inside. The man had been right about the cabin. It was perfectly livable. The roof didn't leak. The wind didn't whistle through too many cracks between the logs, and the fireplace drew as well as any. Arlie Puckett decided that the fire was getting too low, and he bent to toss on another log.

Charlie Summers, sitting on the bed, slipped his revolver out from under the pillow and cocked it. He pointed its muzzle at Puckett's back. Skeeter's eyes grew large.

"You know, Skeeter," said Summers, "I said I'd let you know when the right time come along."

Skeeter grinned wide and pulled his own revolver out of his belt.

"Yeah," he said.

"Keep quiet," said Summers.

Puckett, suddenly curious about the conversation taking place behind him, turned. Red Jack had picked up a rifle by then, and Puckett found himself looking three guns in the barrels.

"Don't try nothing, Arlie," said Summers. "We ain't got nothing against you. You keep quiet, you won't get hurt. Skeeter, get his gun from him."

Puckett, his mouth hanging open, slowly raised his hands, and Skeeter reached out with his left hand to get Puckett's revolver.

"Good," said Summers. "Now Jack, you watch out that window to see when old

Thane's coming back. Let me know."

Red Jack moved to a window and peered out cautiously.

"You going to kill Thane?" said Puckett.

"Just keep quiet," said Summers.

"Here he comes," said Red Jack.

Summers turned his revolver away from Puckett and aimed at the door. Skeeter did the same. Red Jack was still watching the window.

"He's coming around the house now," he said.

"Get ready," said Summers.

Red Jack aimed his rifle at the door. There was a long, tense moment of silence. Then they heard the snow crunching under the footsteps of Thane Savage. The door opened, and Savage stepped in. He was looking down, stamping his feet to get the snow off his boots. Summers pulled the trigger, and a slug tore into Savage's mid-section. Savage looked up, astonished.

He grabbed for the wound, and blood ran out between his fingers. Then Skeeter fired into Savage's chest. Savage staggered back, then forward, then dropped on his knees. Eyes wide, he looked from one man to the other. He was staring in disbelief at Arlie Puckett when Red Jack sent a rifle bullet into his forehead.

Skeeter gave a yell of joy and jumped up and down around the room.

"That's enough," said Summers.

"You going to kill me, too?" asked Puckett.

"That all depends on you," said Summers. "I told you, we got nothing against you. Is there any reason we can't all be friends?"

"No," said Puckett. "There ain't no reason. I ain't got nothing against you. I ain't got nothing against any of you."

"He was your buddy," said Skeeter, accusing.

"I rode with him," said Puckett. "That's all. Hell, you did, too. All of us did."

"Drag him out and around back," said Summers.

"Sure," said Puckett. "I'll get him out of here. Sure."

Puckett moved to the doorway and took the body of Thane Savage by the legs. He dragged it out the door and through the snow, headed for the corner of the cabin. Summers turned to Red Jack.

"Follow him around back and shoot him," he said.

Chapter

20

The cabin was just ahead. Dhu and Barjac both saw it at the same time. Neither spoke. They looked at each other, moved to the side of the road, and dismounted. Each pulled out a rifle. After a moment of hesitation Barjac spoke.

"Well, Walker, what now?"

"You're the expert, Barjac," said Dhu. "You tell me."

"If I was wearing my badge and this was official, we'd get up as close as we could to the cabin, take cover as well as possible, and then I'd holler out. Tell them I'm the law and ask them to surrender."

"And would they?"

"Not likely. They'd probably start shooting."

"So what do you suggest, since you're not wearing your badge?"

"Well, it's pretty cold for it, but I think we'd be better off to hide and watch. They'll come out sooner or later."

"But not necessarily all at once. We might get the first one to come out, but then the others would be alerted."

"Yeah," said Barjac. "That's likely."

Dhu looked up the road toward the cabin. He paced a few limping steps toward it, then turned and paced back. He winced a little with the pain, but he thought that it was probably good for the leg to be working some of the stiffness out of it.

"It's been a long trail, Barjac," he said, "and I'm anxious to get this over with. Besides, I don't like the idea of sitting out here in this cold waiting for them to come out."

"You got any other ideas?"

Inside the cabin the three Arkansas whiskey runners had just finished a meal. Charlie Summers got up, walked over to the bed, and sprawled out on it on his back. The other two still sat at the table.

"Charlie," said Skeeter, "how long we going to set here in this place?"

"I don't know yet," said Summers.

"What'd we follow that damn Texan up here for anyway? Just what the hell are we doing here?"

"We strung along with him thinking we

was going to do some bank jobs," said Summers. "He never got around to planning any, and we got fed up with him. That's all. Now we're here, we just got to make the best out of it. I don't know what to expect of this winter up here."

"What do you mean?"

"I mean what if we was to decide to go back south and we left here and a goddamn blizzard hit? That's what I mean."

"You mean we might just have to sit out the whole damn winter in this shack? Just sit here?"

"I don't know yet," said Summers. "I need to think on it."

They sat for a while in uneasy silence, Skeeter pouting. Then Red Jack tilted his head to one side in visible concentration.

"You hear that?" he said.

"What?" said Skeeter.

"Listen," said Red Jack.

Summers sat up on the bed. In another moment the sound of crunching snow became clear to all three.

"Someone's out there," said Skeeter.

"Take a look," said Summers.

Red Jack went to the window and peered out.

"A rider," he said.

"Alone?" asked Summers.

"Yeah. Just the one."

"Coming this way?"

"Yeah."

Summers sprang up and hurried across the room to stand beside Red Jack and look out the window.

"Get your guns," he said. "Get ready."

"What's he doing?" said Skeeter.

"He's just riding on by," said Red Jack.

"That don't make sense," said Summers. "Go out there and find out what he's up to. Ask him who he is."

Red Jack went to the door, rifle in hand. He opened the door and stepped outside. Skeeter shut the door behind him. Summers stayed at the window.

"Hey," shouted Red Jack.

Dhu, already past the cabin, pulled back the reins to stop his horse. He looked back over his shoulder.

"You calling me?" he said.

"You see anyone else out here? What the hell you doing up here?"

"Just riding by," said Dhu. "I've got a place up yonder."

"What kind of place?"

"A claim."

The door opened again, and Summers stepped out to stand beside Red Jack.

"You a gold miner?" he asked.

"Who's wanting to know?" said Dhu.

"We're just trying to be neighborly," said Summers. "That's all. What's your name, neighbor?"

"I don't have time to waste visiting," said Dhu. "Like I said, I'm just riding by."

"It's cold out here," said Summers. "Why don't you light for a spell? Come inside and get acquainted. We got a warm fire and hot coffee."

"No, thanks," said Dhu. He bounced his heels against his horse's sides and started to ride on ahead.

He thought he could feel the hairs on the back of his neck stand out.

"He ain't going to stop," said Red Jack to Summers in a harsh whisper. "You want me to drop him?"

"No," said Summers. "What if he's got some gold hid up there somewhere? Drop his horse."

Red Jack put his rifle to his shoulder, and down the road behind him Barjac stepped out into the road and fired a quick rifle shot. Dhu dived from the saddle, pulling his rifle with him, and rolled for the cover at the edge of the road as Red Jack screamed with pain, dropped his rifle, and clutched at his shoulder. Summers pulled a revolver from his belt and turned

232

toward the new danger. Barjac cranked his rifle and fired again. The bullet crushed Summers's sternum. He stood wavering for a moment, a stupid expression on his face, then he pitched forward to land on his face — dead.

Red Jack was running for the cabin, but Skeeter had stepped into the doorway with his rifle. Dhu fired, and his shot tore away part of Skeeter's face. Skeeter screamed, but he stayed on his feet and fired two wild shots. Then a shot from Barjac dropped him. Red Jack stopped, confused. He looked toward Dhu, then toward Barjac. He turned back toward the door and looked down at Skeeter lying there.

"Give it up," called Barjac.

Red Jack hesitated another moment, then reached for the rifle in the dead hands of Skeeter. Barjac and Dhu both fired. Both bullets hit Red Jack. He jerked twice, then fell over dead.

It was suddenly deathly still, and in the silence Dhu was conscious of a renewed throbbing in his leg. There are two more, he thought, but where the hell are they? Could they have gone somewhere and left these three behind? More likely they sent these three out to face the danger, he thought, and they were still inside. He stood up cautiously, gritting his teeth against the pain in his leg, and began inching his way along the edge of the trail, trying his best to keep out of sight of anyone who might be peering out the windows of the cabin.

It seemed to take forever, but he finally managed to work his way up to the cabin, and he ran for the near wall, throwing his back against it. He could feel the blood running down his leg. All this sudden activity had caused the wound to start bleeding again.

There was still no sign of life inside the cabin. There was a window in the wall, but he did not want to look through it. Anyone inside would have him framed perfectly for an easy shot.

He scooted along the wall toward the back of the cabin. Then he peered around the corner. There were two bodies lying stiffly there in the snow.

Dhu straightened up and hobbled over to the bodies for a closer look. When he saw the face of Thane Savage he felt suddenly empty. He stood staring at the wretched, lifeless form for a long moment, and he took several deep breaths of cold mountain air. Then he made his halting way around the cabin to the trail. The leg wound seemed to bother him more as soon as the situation was no longer desperate.

"Come on over," he called out to Barjac. "They're all dead."

Back in his own office, his badge back on his chest, Barjac poured a cup of coffee and handed it to Dhu. Then he poured another for himself. He took the cup and walked back around his desk to sit down.

"How's the leg doing, Walker?" he asked.

"It's better," said Dhu. "It's coming along. Thanks."

"Well, where do you go from here?"

"Oh, I think I'll just head back for Texas," said Dhu. "You know, I think I learned something from all this."

Barjac sipped his coffee and waited for Dhu to continue.

"It took me getting a long ways off from home to realize that I really do have a home. Well, I'm going back to it. There's a woman there, too. If she's still waiting for me, I'll marry her — if she'll have me."

"That sounds like a good idea to me," said Barjac.

"Another thing," said Dhu. "And I guess you'd call this learning the hard way. I rode all this way, took all this time out of my life, got shot, risked getting killed, I guess, all to get Thane Savage. When I found him he was already dead. My people, the Cherokee, always said that a man gets back what he dishes out. If I had really believed that, I could have saved myself all this."

"It does kind of look that way," said Barjac. "But it seems to me that sometimes somebody has to help them get it back."

"I don't know," said Dhu. "I don't know."

"So when will you start?"

"Well, I guess I'll spend a night here in your town. First thing in the morning I'll head south. And I think I'll stop over in the Cherokee Nation for a while. I've done some killing. I think I need to see a Cherokee doctor. I think I need some purifying before I go home to my friends to stay."

Epilogue

A weary Dhu Walker sat on his horse in front of the home of Yellow Hammer. It was cold, but not nearly so much as it had been in the country far to the north. He was glad to be back in the Cherokee Nation. But he realized, a little surprised, that it would feel even better to be back at the LWM in Texas.

The door to the cabin opened. Someone was peering out to see who had arrived. In another moment Yellow Hammer stepped out, a wide grin on his face.

"*'Siyo*," he said. "You've had a long journey. Welcome back."

"*Wado*," said Dhu.

"Come in," said Yellow Hammer. "It's cold out here."

Dhu swung down out of the saddle, tied his horse, and followed Yellow Hammer into the cabin. The "knower" poured some coffee into a tin cup and handed it to Dhu.

"*Wado*." Dhu sipped the coffee. "It's good," he said.

"You found what you were looking for?" asked Yellow Hammer.

"Yes," said Dhu. "I did."

"And now you're back? Are you just passing by?"

Yellow Hammer's house was too far out of the way for anyone to be "just passing by." Dhu knew that, and he knew that Yellow Hammer knew it, too. It was just the knower's roundabout way of asking Dhu why he had come.

"Uncle," said Dhu respectfully, "I killed some men. I followed them for a long ways, and then I killed them. Now I want to go home."

Yellow Hammer had known what Dhu wanted. He took him to another cabin not far away. "My daughter's house," he said, and there, with a number of others, they had a big meal. Yellow Hammer kept telling Dhu to eat more.

"It's the last you'll have until two nights from now. Two nights and part of another day."

Dhu ate until he could not force another bite down. He thought that he might be sick, but he managed to avoid that embarrassment. He moved slowly and carefully until he went to bed back at Yellow Hammer's house that night.

He woke up the next morning to the sound of Yellow Hammer singing in a soft, low voice. He couldn't make out any of the words. He got up and dressed himself. Soon Yellow Hammer had stopped singing. He greeted Dhu.

"It's already started," he said. "If any women happen to come by, don't speak to them. Don't speak to any woman until we're all done here. And don't eat anything."

That first day Dhu wondered just what was going on. He wasn't doing anything but sitting around getting hungry. Now and then Yellow Hammer would sing a song, and now and then he mixed something in a bowl. Dhu knew better than to try to hear the words or try to see what the knower was doing, and Yellow Hammer didn't tell him anything.

About the middle of the day Yellow Hammer filled the bowl of a short stemmed clay pipe and lit it. He puffed on it a few times and handed it to Dhu to smoke. They passed it back and forth until it was all smoked up. Dhu went to bed that night almost in agony from hunger, and he had a throbbing headache.

The next day was much the same as the first, except by the middle of the day, when they smoked the pipe again, the headache was gone. He was still hungry, but the pain from the hunger was dull. He knew then that he could stand it. That night he slept reasonably well.

The third morning, when Dhu crawled out of bed, he felt weak. Yellow Hammer was singing again. Dhu sat around most of the morning feeling listless. About noon Yellow Hammer again produced the pipe, and again they smoked together. Then Yellow Hammer put some kind of mixture onto a fire to cook. After it had boiled he poured some into the tin cup from which Dhu had earlier had coffee.

"Come with me," said Yellow Hammer.

He led the way to the edge of the woods a short way off from the house. Then he offered the cup to Dhu.

Dhu took it and looked at it. It was filled with a steaming black liquid. It had the appearance of strong coffee.

"Drink it," said Yellow Hammer, and Dhu turned up the cup and drank it down. It was hot and bitter, and it seemed to start churning when it hit Dhu's stomach. He flinched from a sudden spasm in his guts, and as he grabbed for his middle he dropped the tin cup.

He winced with pain from the convulsions that followed, and he dropped to his knees. Then he felt the contents of his stomach start to roil, and he fell forward, catching himself on his hands, letting the vile liquid take its course.

Back at the LWM Dhu gave himself a few days to get back into the swing of things, to get used to a normal life again, to get back in tune with the rhythms of a working day, but most of all, to get used to being around his friends and to get them used to him again.

After supper one evening he managed to get Ben alone. They sat on the porch in front of Ben's house, and Dhu rolled himself a cigarette and offered the makings to Ben. Ben took them and rolled himself one. Then Dhu struck a match and lit both smokes. They sat for a moment smoking in silence.

"It's good to have you back, buddy," said Ben.

"Ben," said Dhu, afraid that someone would come out of the house unexpectedly and interrupt a conversation that he meant to keep private, "let's take a walk."

Without waiting for an answer he stood up and started to stroll down the long stretch of lane that led to his own small house. Ben followed, curious. The sun was low in the western sky. Soon it would be dark.

"Ben," said Dhu.

"Yeah?"

They walked along a few more steps in silence.

"What?" said Ben.

Dhu stopped walking and tossed away what was left of his cigarette. He did not turn to face Ben.

"What is it?" said Ben. "You ain't fixing to take off on us again, are you?"

"No," said Dhu, "I'm not. You know, Ben, I don't think I ever want to leave this ranch again."

"Really?" said Ben. "You mean that?"

"Well, it's — it's like home."

"Hot damn, Dhu. Everybody's going to be glad to hear that."

"You think so?"

"Hell, I know. We talked about it while you were gone. Everyone missed you. Come on. Let's go back and tell them."

Ben turned to hurry back to the main house, but Dhu grabbed him by the arm.

"Wait a minute," he said. "Hold on."

Ben turned back to face Dhu. He wrinkled his face in puzzlement. "Dhu," he said, "you got something on your mind?"

"Yes. I do. That's why I brought you out here to talk. Damn it."

"Well then, talk. What is it anyway?"

"It's not that easy," said Dhu.

Suddenly Ben felt strange. He felt a kind of reversal of roles. Dhu Walker was having a difficult time telling him something. That had never happened before. Usually Dhu had little to say, and when he did it was to tell Ben to do something or to keep quiet.

"You in some kind of trouble, Dhu?" he asked. "You got the law after you or something for killing them bastards up north?"

"Ben, will you shut up?" said Dhu. "It's nothing like that. And how can I figure out what to say with you going on the way you are?"

"Well, what do you want me to do? You want me to just stand here until you figure out what to say?"

"Yes," said Dhu. "That's exactly what I want you to do."

He pulled the makings out of his pocket and rolled another smoke. Then he held them out toward Ben.

"I don't want none," said Ben. "I'm just standing here, that's all."

Dhu stuffed the makings back into his pocket and produced a match, which he struck on the seat of his pants. He lit his smoke and took a deep drag. Then he slowly expelled the smoke into the cool night air.

"Ben," he said, "I want to ask you something. If your father was alive, I'd be asking him. But he's not. So I have to ask you."

He took another drag on the cigarette, and he paced away from Ben.

"What the hell do you want?" said Ben. "You know, it's getting cold out here."

Dhu turned fast to face Ben again.

"I want to marry your sister, damn it," he said. Both men stood silent, facing each other, stunned. "I want to ask you," said Dhu, more slowly, a little more composed, "if I can ask her if she'll marry me."

There was another long and awkward pause, and then Ben burst into laughter. Finally he got control of himself again.

"That's it?" he said. "That's what this was all about?"

"That's it," said Dhu.

"Well then, sure. Ask her."

Dhu breathed a heavy sigh of relief. "You don't mind?" he said.

"No," said Ben. "Hell, no. Go on ahead and ask her."

"All right," said Dhu. "I will."

They started walking back toward the main house. Ben chuckled. "I never seen you have so much trouble getting anything out," he said.

"Ben," said Dhu. "What do you think she'll say?"

"I know what she ought to say," said Ben, a smile on his lips. "She ought to slap your face and tell you to go to hell because you ain't good enough for her. That's what she ought to say. But that ain't what she's going to say. I know what she'll say."

"Well?" said Dhu.

"She's going to say, 'Hell, yes!' " said Ben. "That's what she'll say. Come on. Let's get on back."

Ben ran ahead, excited. Dhu stood for a moment watching him. He took a final drag on his smoke and tossed it away. He was glad to have that conversation out of the way, and he was anxious to get started on the next one, the one in which he would ask Katharine to be his wife. Yes, indeed, it felt good to be home.

We hope you have enjoyed this Large Print book. Other Thorndike, Wheeler or Chivers Press Large Print books are available at your library or directly from the publishers.

For more information about current and up-coming titles, please call or write, without obligation, to:

Publisher
Thorndike Press
295 Kennedy Memorial Drive
Waterville, ME   04901
Tel. (800) 223-1244

Or visit our Web site at:
www.gale.com/thorndike
www.gale.com/wheeler

OR

Chivers Press Limited
Windsor Bridge Road
Bath BA2 3AX
England
Tel. (01225) 335336

Or visit the Chivers Web site at:
www.chivers.co.uk

All our Large Print titles are designed for easy reading, and all our books are made to last.